Romantic Times: Vegas

Pamela Morsi

Linda J. Parisi

Jeff DePew

Lori Avocato

Connie Corcoran Wilson

Mathew Kaufman

C. H. Admirand

Christina Skye

13Thirty Books
Print and Digital Editions
Copyright 2016

Discover new and exciting works by 13Thirty Books at
www.13thirtybooks.com

Print and Digital Edition, License Notes

ISBN: 0692667210
ISBN-13: 978-0692667217

DEDICATION

To all the amazing people at Romantic Times who over the years have changed so many lives in so many positive ways.

CONTENTS

ACKNOWLEDGMENTS

Judy Spagnola
For all her hard work in making this anthology possible.

And to
Rick Taubold for his editorial assistance.

FOREWORD

Kathryn Falk, Lady of Barrow

Kisses and hugs to 13Thirty Books for compiling a Romance Anthology: *Romantic Times: Vega*s, to entertain the readers at the 33rd RT Booklovers Convention 2016 in Las Vegas.

The lineup of authors is quite varied and impressive, starting with my longtime friend, **Heather Graham**, author of over 150 romances and thrillers. She began writing Romance novels at the same time I started a tabloid publication, *Romantic Times*, now *RT Book Reviews*, and the Booklovers Convention—despite people saying I was crazy to do so.

Several name authors in this collection were also involved in the early days of the Romance genre. It was a much different industry then, smaller and less chaotic. We pushed a lot of envelopes with our stories.

Christina Skye was a Chinese scholar and spoke fluent Mandarin when she appeared on the scene and expressed a desire to write Regencies.

Carole Nelson Douglas, a prominent journalist, stayed in the St. Paul Pioneer Press office till after midnight to help the Romance cause by placing a story of the RT Love Train on the "wires," as it was called in those days. This activated nation-wide coverage for the dozens of authors aboard Amtrak, greeting romance readers (dressed in pink) at stations large and small as we headed from Los Angeles to meet up with Barbara Cartland at the 2nd RT Booklovers Convention in New York City.

Who can forget when contemporary author **Tina Wainscott** arrived at a Convention straight from Russia—having finally succeeded in adopting a baby girl (now 13 years old)—to share her happiness and tins of Russian caviar with her delighted sister authors.

Last but not least, there's no one like our romantic publishers: **Lance Taubold** was one of RT's first cover model contestants, from the Fabio days, as well as being a wonderful singer/entertainer. **Rich Devin** masterfully directed many RT Cover Model Pageants and Awards Ceremonies. It would not be the same biz without them!

RT is fortunate to have loyal friends who are still supporting us after three decades! Ken, Carol, and I are very lucky in this regard and so appreciative.

How romantic it is to come together now *under the covers*, (Sorry for the pun!) and to be writing stories about romantic times in Las Vegas.

Readers will be pleasantly surprised to recognize the names of three prominent authors of Romance who disappeared from the scene for a few years, but have returned to contribute to this collection: Rebecca Paisley, Doris Parmett, and Kimberly Cates.

The three anthologies are rounded out by a talented group of "relatively" new newcomers, including a Barnes & Noble bookseller/author—Crystal Perkins.

A huge thank you to all the authors who brought their imagination and creativity to produce the first RT Convention Anthologies.

To understand how the project developed. Every author received these directives from the publisher:

1) Write a story set in Las Vegas with action taking place inside an imaginary hotel, the Excelsior, built in 1960 by a Mafia family. (That was rather common in those days.)

2) Choose a time frame ranging from 1960 to the present, and even the future, in any genre.

Therefore, dear reader, you will encounter—at the Excelsior

Hotel—a vampire, a post-apocalyptic romance, a time-travel suspense, a Fabio-to-the-Rescue comedy and more...

All our Romances have happy endings of course. And the Romance formula even in short fiction will ring true—getting an alpha male to commit!

Enjoy!

Kathryn Falk, Founder of RT Book Reviews and the RT Booklovers Convention

Kenneth Rubin, President of Romantic Times Inc. (He slept his way to the top!)

Carol Stacy, Publisher and Executive Convention Director

1

EX-SIGHTING

Pamela Morsi

February 2016

Regina Hurley had always imagined that one of the expectations of sitting at a bar in Vegas would be a very genuine anonymity. Never mind that in those Sex and the City episodes she'd watched in high school, Carrie Bradshaw accidently ran into Big a half dozen times. Manhattan was not Vegas. No running in high heels on the sidewalks. Way too hot.

She'd only been back in the country for two months and the new stateside job was an adjustment. Years of travel meant no friends or acquaintances outside of work. Which was why she was sitting alone at the bar in the Excelsior Hotel. The place appealed to her. With its woody paneling and the Louvre print over the back of the bar, a girl could almost expect the Rat Pack to drop in for some debonair crooning. It was somehow so American. Strangely, she had missed that. She was not quite ready to go to her room, but too tired to actually go out. So she sat munching on lamb meatballs in sofrito and sipping a nice shiraz.

She was only vaguely aware of a couple entering when she heard her name voiced in surprise.

"Regi?"

She looked up into eyes that were almost as familiar to her as her own.

Ten years is a long time. A very long time to not have contact with a childhood playmate, to lose track of a high school sweetheart, to miss a best friend. Ten years is a nanosecond when it comes to someone that you left standing at the altar.

"Jake!"

She stared at him stupidly. She was desperately tamping down the need to run screaming for the door. It was Jake Wilkins standing right next to her. The Jake Wilkins that she'd been successfully avoiding for an entire decade.

"What are you doing here?" he asked. "Last I heard you were in London."

That was two years ago.

"I'm here on business," she answered.

"Me too. Plumbing supply convention."

"You're still working for your dad's company?"

He shrugged, but managed a smile. "Dad's retired. My company now."

"Of course."

Regi tried to look away, but realized she was starved for the sight of him. He had changed, but maturity looked good on him. The dark brown hair was cut neater, shorter than it had been in college. The tall skinny body of his teenage years seemed to have filled out very attractively. Dressed in an expensively tailored suit with the modern fit preferred by movie actors because it emphasized a trim waist, he looked, fit, muscular, drop dead gorgeous, in fact. Her mouth went so dry she gulped the shiraz.

"You look great," he said. "You look... you look wonderful."

Regi wasn't so sure. She'd been working in her room all day. She'd only gotten out of her pajamas an hour ago and couldn't remember if she'd combed her hair or put on her makeup.

"Thanks."

At that moment she noticed that he was not alone. Beside him, a very pretty blond woman with a lithe figure and doe-like eyes was gazing at her in astonishment, her mouth rounded into an O.

"Regina? Regina Hurley? Oh my God! I don't believe it. It's you. It's really you!" The young woman actually squealed and tried clumsily to hug her. "You probably don't remember me. Lainey, Lainey Gwiesel, or I used to be. I'm Puff's kid sister. I used to try to hang out in your vicinity. You were my teenage role model." She giggled with delightful enthusiasm.

Lainey Gwiesel. Regi did remember Lainey Gwiesel. She was a skinny, stringy-haired kid, who followed her like a shadow. The only thing about that Lainey that wasn't totally flat was her giant buckteeth covered by shiny braces. This woman was soft, curvy, with a beautiful smile and a clever cut hairdo. She was two, maybe three years younger, but those differences are huge in high school.

Stating the obvious, "You're all grown up," Regi said.

She laughed. "Way too grown up," she replied. "I've got two little ones upstairs."

"Really? Two kids."

She nodded. "Two stubborn, opinionated little terrors. They are Wilkins brothers through and through. Bickering all day long and completely inseparable."

"Don't listen to her," Jake said. "They are the sweetest little guys ever. More like their mama than their dad or uncle."

"I'm sure Regi doesn't detect even a hint of bias in that." She smiled broadly at her before she turned to Jake. "I'm going to go up and order room service."

"I thought you wanted a drink," he said.

Lainey shook her head. "I was only keeping you company," she answered. "Now you can stay here with Regi and catch up."

"Oh, okay," he answered.

Lainey reached over and took Regina's hand. "It was so great to see you. Don't be a stranger. You still have plenty of friends in Cossville."

"Thank you."

The woman then turned a dazzling smile on Jake and gave his arm a familiar squeeze.

Regi watched the woman walk away and found herself struggling against the inexplicable urge to cry. Of course he would be married. He was a getting-married kind of guy. He always had been.

He'd always wanted to marry Regi.

It was meant to be the biggest social event the town had ever seen. The First Methodist Church was stuffed to the rafters with white bows and floral displays. Everybody who was anybody was seated in the pews. And all those who'd managed to remain un-notable were there as well, making it a very tight fit. The town's two most prominent families were being united in marriage. But it wasn't simply that. Regi Hurley and Jake Wilkins, top students in class, were both friendly and popular. Regi and Jake. Jake and Regi. They were like salt and pepper. Like ham and eggs. No one ever thought of them separately, it was always together. Maybe that was why they were chosen "Cutest Couple" in the high school's yearbook three years in a row.

They'd been going steady since the summer before freshman year. He'd given her a promise ring on the night of Senior Prom. They'd gotten officially engaged over a spring break vacation in college and now, both graduates with bright futures, the vows were exactly what everyone expected.

So it had come as quite a surprise when Regina Hurley, in a flowing gown of pure white, full-length veil and eight-foot train, stood on her father's arm at the entry to the sanctuary. She gazed down the aisle at the man she loved and then turned to her dad and said, "I can't do this. Get me out of here."

"Gin and tonic," Jake said to the bartender as he seated himself on the stool next to her. "How have you been?" he asked, conversationally. "Since your parents retired to the lake, I don't get much news about you anymore."

Had people given him news about her? Regi was surprised by that. She'd always discouraged her family from even mentioning his name. Perhaps because all they ever told her was how sad and lost and heartbroken he was. She'd felt guilty enough. She didn't need reminders of how she'd hurt him. So she'd stopped the flow of information.

"It really is a great surprise to catch you here alone at the bar. I hope I'm not intruding," he said. "Were you waiting on someone?"

"Not anyone in particular," she answered.

He gave her a little half smile of confusion.

Regi deliberately kept her expression serene. She was not going to have him thinking that her life had turned into a series of lonely evenings drinking in bars. "Those of us who travel for business get to

4

know each other," she told him, honestly. "Once you've been delayed in Delhi for seventeen hours, you feel like those with you are friends."

He nodded and smiled. She loved that smile.

"So is it still exciting, all those new places and new people?"

Regi shrugged. "Honestly, it's a job," she told him. "Some days it's the best job in the world, and some days it's all I can do to keep going. I'm sure working in your business is a lot like that too."

"Fair enough," he agreed.

He tapped his fingernails absently on the bar.

She took a sip of wine. The silence lingered between them.

"She's lovely, by the way," Regi said.

His brow momentarily furrowed. "Who? Oh, Lainey. Yeah, she's turned out to be a nice looking woman. I remember when I used to think she was like a capital L. Straight up and down, but with very long feet."

Regi managed a smile. "And two kids... wow."

"Yeah, amazing, huh. And she's a good mom. She does payroll for the company and has never missed a day of work. Brought the babies as newborns to the office. I went charging in there one day to ask a question and got a big surprise. She's sitting at her desk, typing one handed with a baby at her breast."

They laughed together and Regi stifled an unwelcome stab of jealousy.

His drink showed up and he stirred it with the straw.

"I still find it hard to believe that you're married with a family and nobody ever said a word."

A strange look crossed his face and Regi realized how that must have sounded.

As if she expected him to carry a torch for her forever. To pine away in love for her, like she was the only woman in the world. To feel forever that a piece of him had been torn away, never to heal.

The way that she felt.

Clearly, Jake had moved on.

*

When he'd seen her sitting at the bar he couldn't believe it, then he couldn't breathe. His first instinct was to pull her into his arms.

Thankfully, he didn't do that. He didn't really know what he did. He muttered something about the convention and the business, but he could hardly hear his own words over the alarm bells going off in his head.

She was here. She was here, now. She was here with him. So many times he'd prayed for it. So many nights he'd dreamed of it. Now suddenly, unexpectedly, it was happening. And he couldn't even think.

Fortunately, Lainey sailed into the breach. Unfailingly cheery and chatty, his sister-in-law was enough of a distraction to allow him to get a rein on headlong rush of his heart. He composed himself. Pulled his fantasies back into reality. Regi had not coming running back to him. He had only run into her. He could not react as if she were the love of his life. She was a near stranger, who he had once known so very, very well.

When Laney left, he seated himself at the barstool beside her and followed her lead into small talk. She was vaguely smiling, so he wasn't sure if she was interested or just polite. He got her to laugh. It was a sound he remembered. Their love had been rife with laughter.

"I still find it hard to believe that you're married with a family."

For a microsecond he was clueless about what she meant. Then the truth flooded in with incredulity. Regi thought Lainey was married to him.

His first impulse was to set her straight, but he didn't. Something silenced his voice long enough to think of the long game. Maybe it was better this way. If he wasn't available, she couldn't reject him. And if she couldn't reject him, then he could relax and truly enjoy this unexpected gift of time with her.

"What about you?" he asked, instead. "Have you settled on one of these international road warriors for happily ever after?"

She laughed, but it sounded a bit self-conscious. "You know me," she pointed out. "Marriage is not really my thing."

He laughed along with her and was glad that they could laugh together.

"Relationships on the road are very different." She held her chin high, her demeanor almost defensive. "There's not really any 'dating' as such. You meet up with someone, you enjoy their company, and maybe you hook up. In the morning you both feel great and he heads off to Beijing, while you catch a plane to Bucharest."

There was a lot of deliberate casualness in her words that suggested a jaded carnality with which he was unfamiliar. If he spent the night with her, he'd never make it to China.

Her attitude might be new, but the rest of her was much how he remembered. The long chestnut hair that used to hang to her waist was considerably shorter and pulled off her neck in some kind of loose, twisty thing that emphasized the elegant curve of her jawline. Her figure was, if changed at all, trimmer and more fit than their college days. And her legs, in that short skirt and high heels, still had the power to turn his knees into jelly, and the area higher up into stone.

He looked away and tasted his drink. An awkward moment lingered between them.

"So tell me about your family," she said.

"My folks still live in our house. Dad plays a little golf, but mostly he putters around in the shop, fixing old appliances that he then donates. Mom's taken up painting, and she's actually pretty good at it. I have an Irma Wilkins original oil hanging above the couch in my living room."

"I always liked your parents," she said.

"They always liked you."

Jake loved that smile. It always caught him right in the gut.

"When I asked about your family, I meant Lainey and the kids."

Of course that's what she meant. "Well, you met Lainey," he said. "The kids are… kids."

"I bet they have names and ages," Regi told him.

"Daniel is three. Pete is about a year and a half, maybe."

Her brow wrinkled. "A year and a half, maybe?" she repeated.

"Sixteen months," he guessed randomly. Jake had the actual birthday on his phone, but thought it would be way too suspicious to look it up.

"And you named him after your brother," she said. "You two must have gotten a lot closer."

Jake pushed through his hesitation.

"We are better," he agreed with a nod. "Pete started his own business. He's a commercial contractor. He's done really well and doesn't have to feel like he's always in my shadow these days, always in competition."

Regi nodded. "Good for him. I'm sure it was never easy being

7

the kid brother to the son who always did everything right."

"Not everything."

Jake did not elaborate, but in memory, he saw her once more across the length of the church. He saw the panicked, regretful pallor on her face. With the Bridal March blaring from the organ pipes, he couldn't hear the words she spoke to her father, but he immediately knew what they meant. Maybe if he'd run after her that very minute. But his own guilt made him hesitate. By the time he'd made it to the church door, the long white limo was driving away.

"So did Pete marry? Does he have a family?"

"What?" He pretended not to hear. The bar had filled up noisily around them, making the pretense of deafness believable. "Maybe we can find a quieter table."

With an order for some food of his own and the assistance of a waiter waved in by the bartender, they carried their drinks across the room. Jake would never have had the guts to pick the seats they were led to. It was in a small, secluded niche with a comfy padded loveseat, table in front.

Regi slipped in one side, he on the other, but when they sat their thighs were touching. They smiled at each other, but he knew his was forced and thought hers might be too.

"So, I'm the guy with the boring life in Cossville," he said. "You're the woman who's seen the world. Tell me about the boring life in London or Paris or Rome."

She laughed a little. "I know more about the boring life in Prague and Budapest and Ljubljana. My most successful territory was Eastern Europe. These days, it's all Asia."

Jake leaned an elbow on the table so that he could watch her face as she talked. She had always been like this. So full of life and joy. Always eager to get out into the world, to see those things that she hadn't seen. To meet those people so different from her. Her stories were not about palaces and cathedrals and monuments. She talked about children skating on icy rivers, old women smoking pipes as they did leatherwork, street musicians and food vendors. She loved all of it.

The waiter came with his order and fresh drinks. He had no idea what he was eating, but it tasted great, and he began to really relax. She did too.

This was a time out of time. He was going to savor these

moments with her for many years to come. He might never talk to her again and he realized that there were still words that he had to say.

*

Seated so close to him on the tiny loveseat, Regi told herself that she was very glad that he was married. It made everything so much easier. That he had found happiness without her, absolved her of guilt. Her residual feelings for him, her wish that things could have been different, that was a punishment she deserved.

Still, Regi hadn't been quite as humbled as she knew she should have been. She didn't want him to think that she still sighed with longing at the memory of him. That he was the standard by which she judged other men and that, for her, they never measured up.

So she deliberately spiced her stories of foreign adventure with some broad hints about her sexual exploits. And if she conveyed them to be a bit more exciting than they actually were, well, he would be as gratified to know that he hadn't ruined her life as she was to know she hadn't ruined his.

"So three days in Madrid was one long party," she explained. "Great food, great music and so much dancing. I thought Marco was a bit young for me, but I had plenty of money and he knew how to enjoy himself. Then one afternoon we're looking at art at the Reina Sofia and I hear 'Papa! Papa!' And here are the two cutest little kids on a school field trip."

"Oh no."

"Oh yes." She laughed with exaggerated gaiety. "And the mom was a trip chaperone. I got to meet the whole family."

"Oh God, what did you do?"

"There was nothing to do," Regi told him. "I was charming and friendly and pretended this kind of thing happened every day."

Jake shook his head incredulously, but he was smiling. She wondered if she had shocked him. She wondered if that's what she'd intended.

The incident had happened so very long ago and it had been horrible. She had been so lonely and he had been so full of life. She had grabbed for a heart salve and ended with a handful of humiliation. She could no longer remember the Spaniard's face, but she could never forget the eyes of those children.

9

The warmth of Jake beside her, the scent of him, it was so intoxicating. She didn't want him to leave. She kept chattering in the hope that he would stay.

He switched to wine and had the waiter bring them a bottle.

It seemed very natural to be with him. She had to resist the impulse to snuggle in his arms.

"It all sounds very exciting," he told her.

She nodded, but for the sake of being friends, she also wanted to be truthful. "It is sometimes, but you know the traveling thing gets really old," she said. "I love seeing new places and even revisiting cities that I love. But there is a lot of business to be done in cities and industrial zones that I don't love. And day after day dragging a bag on and off a plane or trying to figure out how to turn the heat on in unfamiliar hotel rooms, that gets old."

Jake smiled. "I guess in the end, a job is a job."

Regi agreed. "And I love what I do," she said. "But these days I find myself doing a lot more of it by video chat and web conferencing."

"That's certainly more efficient and less expensive."

She agreed. "And when a face-to-face is absolutely required, more often than not I'm managing and mentoring younger staff on the road."

"I bet that has its moments too."

Laughingly, she told him about a phone call, explaining the vagaries of parking a rental car on a side street in Seoul.

When he chuckled, Regi noted a bit of five-o'clock shadow on his jaw line. It served as a reminder to her that this man with the polite manners and friendly smiles was still wholly masculine, a fiercely passionate and unrelenting sexual partner.

She swallowed that thought with another splash of Shiraz and began a very recent story about the foibles of a staff member who had an overly optimistic confidence in his language skills. She wanted to hear him laugh. She loved the sound of it pouring over her like a warm balm.

A moment later, Regi looked into Jake's eyes and forgot everything else. Those amazingly long eyelashes, darker than his hair. She used to tease him, saying that he must secretly be using mascara. Once, as a joke, he allowed her to catch him sneaking the tube out of her purse.

And she remembered those eyelashes fluttering against her temple as she awakened in his arms.

For the first time in an hour, there was silence between them. All around them noisy, happy revelers celebrated wins or drank to forget losses, but in the cozy alcove two people gazed at each other.

Jake looked away first.

"I'm glad you got to go after your dream," he said.

Was he glad? she wondered. Was she glad?

"I'm so sorry about what I did to you," she admitted. "I can't imagine what it was like for you at the church, in front of all those people."

Jake shook his head. "I don't even remember the people. All I remember is watching you make your getaway and realizing that I blew it."

Regi was startled at that statement. "You didn't blow it."

"Yes, I did," he said. "I seriously did. I knew all along what you wanted out of life, and I think it's past time that I apologize for almost stealing it away."

"What? Oh no," she said. "You have nothing to apologize for."

"I do. I do," he insisted. "Sometimes I tell myself that I was just young and stupid. But I wasn't that stupid. I was willfully ignorant."

"What do you mean?"

"I knew you," Jake said. "I had listened to your dreams for years. You wanted to travel the world. You wanted to see new things, meet new people. And it wasn't just pie in the sky, 'I-wanna-be-a-rock-star-when-I-grow-up'. I was there when you earned your degree in International Business. I sat beside you reading subtitles in a million foreign films and travelogues. I drilled you on French conjugations and German declensions. Did I really think you were going to use all that in the front office of the Wilkins' Plumbing Supply?"

Regi felt a blush sliding up her neck. Was that what she had thought? The entire time they'd dated, she'd known that he was being prepped to take over his father's business. And while she had talked about all that she would see and might do, he had never wavered from his plan to go into the family business. No. She'd discounted his dream. His dull, responsible, pedestrian dream was no match for hers. She'd convinced herself that because they really loved each other and because what she wanted was so much bigger, he'd get on board.

"Working at Wilkins was never an option that I considered," she admitted now. "It seemed... boring. A job that old people would do."

His expression registered a momentary surprise, then he laughed. "So I guess that in those years when we thought we were learning how to make a life together, we were actually working at cross-purposes."

"Yeah, I suppose so. When I thought about your future, which was rare, I always assumed that despite what your parents wanted, you would go away with me. That we would travel the world for twenty years and then retire to a beachfront villa on the Mediterranean."

"Now that doesn't sound bad," Jake told her. "You should have let me in on the plan. God knows, some days when I'm listening to some long diatribe about how 'they don't make p-traps like they used to, jetting off to the Riviera is mighty tempting."

"It took me a while to realize that you would never leave your folks in the lurch."

His brow furrowed. "Taking over at the store was not something that my parents pushed on me," he said. "It was always what I wanted."

Regi nodded.

"But, I also wanted you."

His words were low and soft. They sizzled through her veins and caused the butterflies in her mid-section to become frenzied.

Later, she couldn't have said if he moved or she did, but an instant later she was in his arms, tasting his lips. It was all there. Everything that had taunted her in loss and buoyed her in reflection. Like muscle memory their bodies knew each other completely and responded without hesitation. It was as if a fire that never truly cooled suddenly flamed up between them.

Regi knew that she should stop. She knew that for the sake of her heart and her sanity, she couldn't go through it all again.

But just one more minute.

One more minute.

She wanted him. She had always wanted him. And knowing that they were so good together, knowing how thoroughly he could satisfy her, knowing that she might never get another moment to feel him inside her, Regi could so easily give in.

And Jake would never forgive himself.

*

When finally she broke the kiss, he held her face in his hands, inches from his own. Her eyes were bright with passion and her lips plumped and parted. She had never looked more beautiful. He had never wanted her, wanted any woman, more than he wanted her now.

"I thought I had imagined it," she whispered. "I was sure that the spark between us couldn't have been true. But it's still there."

"It's still there," he agreed and pulled her into his arms once more.

Open-mouthed, he angled his head to bring them even nearer to each other. It was as if she were trying to crawl inside him. He sucked the warmth of her into him and nipped her lower lip with his teeth. The sounds she made at the back of her throat were raw and eager. Jake couldn't get close enough. In the tiny, confined space he eased her onto his lap. She pressed her breast against him. He ran a hand down the length of her spine.

"Good grief! Get a room!"

Jake looked up, startled.

His brother, Pete, stood at the edge of their table, grinning.

Regi gasped in horror and abruptly plopped herself back on the seat.

"Hi Regi. You're looking pink and pretty, as always."

"Pete."

"What are you doing here?" Jake demanded.

"Lainey was so nervous about you being with Regi, she couldn't calm down enough to go to sleep. I told her she was nuts, but you know what a romantic she is." Pete chuckled. "She sent me down here on secret reconnaissance. I wasn't supposed to let you see me. But, then I expected you to be chatting civilly and sipping Singapore Slings, not publicly snogging in a dark corner."

"Oh my God, Jake, I am so sorry."

"It's fine."

"It's not fine. Oh, poor, Lainey. Pete, please, please. I'm begging you. It was all my fault. Please don't say anything to her."

"Huh?"

"Jake would never be unfaithful. He's not that kind of guy. It

13

was a moment of craziness. I lured him into the past. I made him remember when he loved me. It was so wrong of me, and I am very sorry. I am so, so sorry." She looked at him then, and Jake saw the same look he'd seen that long ago day in the church. She loved him, but she was going to run. "I know back then I was selfish. I wanted what I wanted and I didn't care who I hurt. But I'm not like that anymore. I do want you, but I won't allow myself to hurt you and your whole family."

She slipped out the far side of the booth, grabbed her purse and headed out the door.

Jake rushed to follow her.

"What's going on?" Pete asked. "What is she talking about?"

"She thinks Lainey and the kids belong to me."

Pete was incredulous. "You told her you're married! Are you a complete idiot?"

"I hope not."

Jake raced at the door. He looked left and didn't see her. He looked right and didn't see her. For an instant he felt complete panic, but he was not hesitating as he'd done at the church. He ran down the hallway toward the elevators. He heard the "ding" before he rounded the corner. She was getting on.

"Stop!" he called out.

She turned to look at him. There were tears in her eyes, but she made no move to hold the door. The shiny metal was closing so quickly. She would be on the other side, maybe lost to him forever.

"I love you! Don't leave me!" he cried out.

Suddenly, from within the car an arm encased in gold lame grabbed the door. A tall, dark man with a slick pompadour and sunglasses looked out at him. "I know only fools rush in, but I think this has to be one of those now or never exceptions."

Jake stepped into the elevator. The Elvis impersonator stepped out. "I'll catch the next one," he said.

When the doors closed behind him. Jake took Regi's hands in his own. "I hesitated ten years ago," he said. "I should have run behind the limo. I should have never let you go. Today, I'm not letting you go."

Tears were running down her cheeks. "You have to. It's too late for us. We have our own lives, our own responsibilities. It could never work."

"It's not too late. We're in love with each other. And we have been for most of our lives. Being in love doesn't mean being free from complications. Being in love means working through those complications together. Being in love doesn't mean having the same goals, it means having the one mutual goal of supporting each other."

"But Lainey and the children…"

"Are now, and have always been, the happy responsibility of my brother, Pete."

"What?"

"There is only one woman in the world that I have ever wanted to marry." He reached over and hit the emergency STOP button. The sudden halt was jarring, but he was on his own power when he got down on one knee. "Marry me, Regi. I don't care if we live in Cossville or Calcutta, but I don't want to live anywhere without you beside me."

*

The midnight to morning hours on the concierge desk at the Excelsior Hotel were typically slow, and during weekdays handled by the nightshift bell captain. His experience with wedding arrangements was slight, but he managed pretty well. Even for a hurry-up, middle of the night occasion, he was able to provide a beautiful bouquet, a sober minister and a cluster of cupcakes with a bride and groom figurine on top. The jeweler at Caesars Palace had sent over a ring by taxi. And a 24-hour rental shop had managed a lovely white gown and veil, as well as the tux. Esperanza from the housekeeping staff was drafted into sitting with two sleeping children while the best man and matron of honor attended the ceremony.

The Excelsior, being a busy, much beloved and historical hotel, held claim to many innumerable "firsts" in its past. But to everyone's recollection, and some searching of the special occasion logs, this was the only wedding ever to take place in their elevator.

2

THE PROMISE

Linda J. Parisi

Excelsior Hotel, Las Vegas, 1962

Love. Funny how such a small word could mean so many different things.

Mac's hand gripped hers, making Sarah intensely aware of the ring he'd just slipped on her finger. "Oh, Mac," she whispered, squeezing back.

Take for instance, the difference between a man and a woman, she thought. For a man, love was the golden crown that made a man a king, the crown he wore with pride for all the world to see. For a woman love was deeper, like the layers of a peacock, splendid in full bloom, shimmering even when hidden.

"Well, Mrs. McDonald?"

All around them the lobby of the Excelsior bustled. Bellboys in bright red uniforms trimmed in gold carried in luggage followed by men in suits and women in mink. But Sarah only saw her husband, so handsome in his gray-blue dress uniform. "I can't believe this is finally happening. Married. Finally."

Sarah gazed up at Mac, hiding none of her feelings for him. His half-quirk, mostly devil-may-care grin made her fall in love with him all over again. For a brief second, she floated back to that moment when they first met. An interesting word, met. Better to say, when she barreled into his rock-hard body ending up in a heap at his feet. As he helped her up, his grin melted her for the first time. She forgot about her chemistry exam. He forgot about the blind date with her sorority sister. They spent the rest of the evening just talking…

His warm kiss on their clasped hands brought her back to the present. Sarah grinned back, shivering as she alternated hot and cold. When she returned the kiss on the back of his hand, heat flared in his gaze, leaving only the remaining embers.

"My very own blond bombshell," he teased.

"I'm not exactly Marilyn Monroe," she was quick to counter.

"No, my beautiful wife. You're my Marilyn Monroe."

Mac picked up her suitcase, hoisted his duffle, and they walked from the entrance of the lobby to the front desk. Bubbling inside with happiness, Sarah wanted to dance and twirl across the floor as if she were a princess at a ball. She fell in love with the hotel immediately. In a town growing with slanted roofs and modern architecture, Sarah slipped into the rich wood and soft tones of the Excelsior with the ease of a glass slipper.

"Lieutenant Michael McDonald. I reserved the honeymoon suite."

The flutter of Sarah's heart battered against the confines of her rib cage.

"Of course, sir. If you'll sign here please?" The desk clerk handed him a key. "The elevator is at the end of the lobby. Top floor."

Sarah caught sight of the patch on his arm. "That Others May Live." The motto thrilled her. But half a world away and to Vietnam, such a dangerous place? She'd read the newspapers. The United States was sending even more "advisors" and becoming even more embroiled in war that wasn't theirs.

With a deep breath, Sarah banished those thoughts immediately. There was only this place. There was only the present.

"Compliments of the house." The clerk slid a couple of chips across the countertop and signaled a bellboy to handle the luggage.

"Congratulations on your marriage."

Mac looped his arm in hers and they followed. But as they reached the casino, he slowed. "Here," he told the bellboy as he pulled out a couple of bills from his pocket. "Take our luggage up to the room." Sara watched wondering what he was doing.

"Yes, sir."

Mac shrugged. "They did give us some chips."

"Boys will be boys?" she teased.

He shook his head and patted her hand. He was giving her time to get used to her new status. Nervous, a little scared, Sarah didn't want to disappoint him. She caught the heat in his gaze and knew exactly why she loved him so much. "Thank you."

Fingers entwined, Mac led her into the casino. Sarah wrinkled her nose at the cigarette smoke as they walked in. Mac brought her to a craps table and a waitress came over to ask if they wanted a drink.

"What do you want, kitten?" he asked, his mouth next to her ear so she could hear. Despite it being the middle of the day, the casino was crowded, almost too crowded for her taste.

"A Manhattan," Sarah replied, trying her best to sound sophisticated, realizing that going to college for three years hadn't quite taken the small town out of the give... yet.

Mac took the opportunity to nip at her earlobe before he placed their order and turned his attention to the craps table. Sarah lost interest quickly and people-watched instead. It was eighty degrees outside yet several women were walking around in mink stoles and hats. Others wore collared no-sleeve shirts and skirts. Her simple, short-sleeved, white A-line dress blended right in, making her not so self-conscious.

Not much of a wedding dress, but then Sarah hadn't known he was going to ship out immediately after graduating flight school. When Mac found out, he proposed, and in less than twenty-four hours, planned a wedding and a honeymoon.

Mac placed a chip on the table. Their drinks came and she sipped, the liquor going straight to her head. Just like Mac.

She watched him play, serious and intense, but that hint of boyishness tugged at her heart. All of a sudden, she noticed people gravitating to the table. Soon they were surrounded. Mac's tie was open, his cap in her hands. He pushed his cupped hands in front of her face and said, "Blow." She did. Hard. Then he called, "C'mon.

Seven."

He made her do it again and then next thing she knew, he was lifting her off her feet and twirling her around. The man with the stick slid a whole pile of chips toward them. "We won!" he cried. "We won!"

As Mac let go, her body slid down his, sparking her desire. He kissed her for all the world to see. His tongue drifted over hers, velvet on velvet. Breathless, Sarah tore her mouth away and downed the rest of her drink to quench the fire. A single brow lifted as Mac confirmed that would be impossible. He gathered the chips, took her hand, and led her to a cashier's window. A thousand dollars!

Grinning from ear to ear he asked, "Well, Mrs. McDonald? What shall we do with it?"

Sarah shook her head, a bit stunned. "I don't know."

They returned to the lobby and Mac stopped dead. Then he said, "C'mon."

He led her back to the front desk. "Do you still have any tickets left for the show tonight, Flower Drum Song?"

The clerk smiled. "As a matter of fact I do. Two. Third row center."

"We'll take them." Mac handed the clerk one of the crisp new hundred dollar bills from the casino. "Keep the change."

Once they were out of earshot she murmured, "Extravagant."

"We can afford it." He tilted his head. There went that grin again. "It's our honeymoon."

Sarah relented and found herself caged between his arms in the elevator. She gazed up at him, her love for him welling in her eyes.

He melted. "Don't cry, kitten. We have the whole weekend ahead of us."

"I'm not sad," she countered. "I'm happy."

His finger trailed down her cheek. She kissed the tip. "Look, I know you're disappointed, that you wanted a big wedding. And we can have one when I come back."

Sarah shook her head. "I don't care about that now. All I care about is you. I love you Mac."

"I love you too, kitten."

As his mouth engulfed hers, Sarah forgot about everything else except this tiny ball of need that raged downhill inside her body growing bigger and bigger as they kissed. Not that they'd been saints, or that they hadn't made out, and then some, but Mac had this definitive idea of right and wrong. He wanted her to be a virgin on their wedding night.

Only it was daytime and the elevator doors were opening.

He grabbed her hand and they practically flew down the hallway. Always the gentleman, he opened the door and then lifted her in his arms to carry her over the threshold. Sarah gasped as he let her feet touch the floor. Six of her bedrooms would fit inside one of these. And the bed? Oh, my!

Sarah couldn't drag her gaze from the cavernous bed. "You won't lose me in there, will you?" she asked with a shaky laugh.

"Never," he replied, his tone beyond serious. He pulled Sarah into his arms. "I love you, Mrs. McDonald."

His gaze deepened, turning those beautiful gray-green eyes nearly emerald. His kisses drugged her, one after the other, until her head spun out of control. She learned from him, exploring his mouth as he explored hers. Then he pulled back and unbuttoned his shirt. Her fingertips slipped down his arms, his skin beading from her touch.

Her turn. His fingers trembled as they undid her buttons, sliding ever so gently across her collarbone and pushing the material away like opening the petals of a flower. Her body reached out to him in a way it never had before, yearning, seeking fulfillment. "I love you too."

"You're so beautiful."

Her fingertips trailed over his chest muscles. "You are too."

After that she drowned in desire, until she found herself nearly naked on the bed with him.

"I've waited so long to love you," he whispered, his mouth drawing a path of fire all over her body.

"I've dreamed of this for… forever."

Her fingers tightened around the back of his neck as his lips engulfed hers. She grew bolder, learning the curves and valleys of his body as he did the same to hers. The floodgates to her yearning begged to open but a tiny shaft of fear kept stabbing at her. She let his kisses mend each tear, until she fell into the spell he weaved. Their clothes long gone, his hips settled between her legs, his weight unfamiliar.

"Kitten?"

She swallowed hard, her chest rising and falling with each deep breath.

"I'll never hurt you. I promise. But I can't do this without—"

She lifted up and kissed him, opening her body, her mind, and her heart until they could go no further. She fell back onto the mattress. "I love you."

"I love you more."

He thrust as gently as he could. There was pain but as she gazed up into his eyes, it became memory. Understanding her wishes, he pulled out and sheathed himself, sliding inside again before she could take her next breath. Then all thought ceased. Nothing existed but the two of them.

Together.

Snuggled deep in his arms, basking in the aftermath, Sarah dozed. When she awoke, his kisses were making her body come alive even more than before. He slipped deep inside her again and this time their lovemaking wasn't about pain, but about pleasure, and the floodgates opened to a raging torrent. And as Sarah came back down to earth, wonder filled her being. Reality was so much better than dreams, she thought, drifting off once more. Mac joined her, snuggling her deep into the crook of his arm.

By the time they awoke again, darkness had fallen.

Sarah stretched, feeling muscles she'd never used before and rose. "Where are you going?" Mac asked, looking adorable and tussled with just a sheet draping his hips.

Sarah laughed. "To the bathroom. And you're going to call for room service while we get dressed. We have show tickets, remember?"

"Forget them," he insisted with a waggle of his brows.

She made a face back at him, an unfamiliar soreness between her legs. "No. I need to... rest."

Sara was never quite sure if it was the lift of his lips that tugged just so at the strings of her heart, or if it was the dimple that deepened by the corner of his mouth. Either way, when he looked at her like that, she'd forgive most anything.

"My apologies, Mrs. McDonald."

Still, it didn't hurt to keep that a secret. "Huh."

He laughed softly and Sarah could feel the heat creep into her cheeks. "Then you'd better shower first," he told her. "I can't swear to my behavior if provoked."

Not quite taking his words to heart, she sat in front of the mirror on the desk, putting on her makeup while he changed into a suit. Watching him, she couldn't quite decide which she preferred, suit or uniform.

Room service arrived. "Hungry?" he asked, the question filled with innuendo.

She answered the visceral one as her stomach growled. "Starving."

They ate, feeding each other bites of a thick rich juicy steak and drinking the complimentary champagne, teasing and laughing all the while.

They reached their seats just before the curtain rose. Transported, Sarah loved every moment of the show. "I can't believe how wonderful it was."

He grinned. "Watching you watch the show was even better. You leaned forward as if you wanted to be on stage right there with them."

"Oh Mac," she breathed.

"Come on. Let's take a walk."

The strip pulsed with a life all its own. Neon glittered everywhere. The glitz and glitter didn't dazzle Sarah. No, she left that for his hazel-green gaze. The people and the sights became a blur and Sarah found herself back at the Excelsior in the Tower Bar sitting at a secluded table in the back, another Manhattan in front of her.

Sara hummed the tune to the show's most captivating song, You Are Beautiful. She felt his gaze on her, her skin rippling with sensation. "What?"

He smiled, that damned dimple showing in his cheek. "I was just thinking how lucky I am."

Was it possible to love too much?

"You think that now," she retorted, grabbing at the last piece of her sanity. For if he took that last tiny vestige of her heart, what would be left? Especially if something happened, if he went missing, if he was… she couldn't even think the word.

In complete and utter self-defense she added, "Wait until I'm fat and a mess and we have two screaming toddlers running around the living room in diapers."

His gaze turned liquid. "I'd love that."

23

She would too, but that was an impossible fairytale. As much as she wanted children, as much as the thought turned her insides to mush, Sarah refused to bring a child into this world without a father. Sipping her drink, she shook her head. "No, Mac. We agreed. Not until you come home. For good. I couldn't bear it if—"

"Hey," he whispered, his knuckle lifting her chin. Tears filled his eyes too. "I told you earlier, these are not allowed. We're on our honeymoon." His thumb wiped away the wetness that escaped down her cheek. "All right. Agreed."

But Sarah knew what he was thinking, what they both were thinking. Very real possibilities loomed over each and every word, each and every heartbeat. He might not come back. Anything could happen. His helicopter could go down in the middle of the jungle. He could be captured by the enemy. A stray bullet could lodge inside his body and he might not come back at all.

They went upstairs and this time they made love with a poignant urgency. Still Sarah refused to give in to that very real, very terrifying possibility. If she did, it would be tantamount to accepting that he might remain in a rice paddy somewhere for eternity. Something Sarah would never do.

*

Sarah slept late the next morning. She awoke to her husband's gaze and smiled. "What time is it?"

"Half past ten."

Sarah stretched with the languid contentment of a cat after a long nap. "So late? Why'd you let me sleep?" Especially when every moment together is so precious, she added to herself.

"Because I loved watching you."

Before she could even voice the thought, he handed her a cup of coffee. After her first sip, she sat up and asked, "What shall we do today?"

He cupped his chin with his hand, making believe he was thinking. "Why not be decadent and lay around the pool a while."

Sarah smiled, knowing that had been a foregone conclusion. "I thought you'd never ask."

"Are you hungry? I left you some toast and eggs, although I'm sure the eggs are cold by now."

"Toast is fine. But first, I need a shower."

Sarah had just stepped into the stall when she felt his hands on her body. Silent as a cat stalking prey, he'd crept up on her, nearly scaring her half to death. And that adrenaline rush created a need greater than any she'd felt. As sweet as the night before had been, this time was different, more visceral, more mating than loving.

His fingers sluiced water and soap down her body. Slick and hungry, his kisses invaded, drawing out the animal in her. And when he kneeled down to pay homage, Sarah wondered where this biting, scratching, out of control woman came from. No longer demure, she gave as good as she got, laughing softly when they came back down to earth on the floor instead of the bed.

They didn't make it down to the pool until early afternoon. By then, shade became the watchword of the day. Mac found them chaise lounges under the awning that bordered the hotel patio, kissed her, and then dove into the pool, his lean muscular body making him stand out among the crowd. Not to be outdone, Sarah stuck her hair in a bathing cap and joined him, though his abilities far exceeded hers.

When he stopped, he swam to her, flinging water right in her face. She reciprocated, laughing. They played in the water a short while then she told him, "I'm going to go relax."

"I need to do a few more laps."

"Better you than me. I'm exhausted."

"Not too exhausted, I hope."

Sarah slapped at his shoulder, swam over to the ladder to get out, and dried off. He kept swimming, a son of Triton. So amazing to watch. And when he lifted himself out of the pool, water glistened on his chest and muscles, and he stood out like a Roman god. Sarah's insides fired on all eight cylinders as he approached, toweling his hair.

"You'd better stop looking at me like that," he said.

"Like what?" she challenged.

"That," he whispered, bending down to kiss her. Water droplets plopped on her thighs. "I think something tall and cold is in order, Mrs. McDonald."

"Indeed."

A woman with red hair sitting in the lounge next to her pulled down her sunglasses. "Honey. Without being so bold. What are you doing down here when you have a hunk like that? Shouldn't you be upstairs?"

Pleased and not put out, Sarah smiled. "We just got married."

"All the more reason," the woman answered. "I hope you don't mind if I stare. I love Gil. But he never, ever, looked like that."

A youngish man with curly brown hair and horned-rimmed glasses came up to them carrying a couple of towels. "Looked like what, dear?"

"Nothing," she murmured. She turned to Sarah. "Lenore... Radovitch. This is my husband Gil."

Sarah held out her hand. "Sarah. Sarah McDonald. The gentleman with the drinks coming toward us is my husband, Michael."

"Hi," he said, handing her a drink. "Call me Mac." He shook hands with both of them. "Can I get you something from the bar?"

"That's not what I'd call you," Lenore murmured. Sara caught the comment, but luckily both men were headed back to the bar to get Gil and Lenore a drink.

"All those muscles." Lenore sighed.

Sarah preened rather than being jealous. "Air Rescue. Helicopter pilot."

"Gil was a sergeant in the Army. Supplies. Now he's an accountant. I'll take it. Especially with the way things seem to be heating up in Southeast Asia."

A part of Sarah wished she was so lucky. For that was exactly where Mac was headed.

"When does he leave?" Lenore asked.

Sarah was surprised by Lenore's astuteness. "We have to be back at base by 17:00 tomorrow."

"How long?"

"A year."

"You poor dear," Lenore remarked, patting her hand.

Sarah drew in a deep breath. "Yes and no. I'm going to finish my degree."

"What are you studying?"

"Biology. I'm going to be a nurse."

"Ladies?" Lenore and Sarah looked up. "Gil and I were just talking," Mac said. "How about we have dinner together tonight?"

Sara tilted her head at her husband. He wasn't one to share. But a little company would help take her mind off their impending departure.

The afternoon passed far too quickly as Sarah found Lenore and Gil to be as entertaining as any comics on the strip. Her sides ached from laughing.

"I hope you folks don't mind but we need to get going," Mac said.

Sarah looked up at Mac, wanting to stay. She rose anyway, hugged Lenore and Gil, the men shook hands and they left.

"What was that all about?" she asked as they made their way to the elevators.

"I need to go to the pharmacy. For—"

"Oh," Sara blushed. "I'll come with you. I need some cream after all that sun."

They dressed and walked along the strip. They went around the corner onto Spring Mountain Road and stepped into the pharmacy. Mac bought what they needed while Sarah spied a photo booth. "Please?"

"Aren't you being a bit corny?" he protested.

She shook her head and crossed her arms over her chest. He relented and they took pictures with her sitting on his lap. Most of them were kisses but a couple were portraits. On the way back to the hotel, Sarah tore the last two off. In one they were facing the camera, in the other they were kissing. "Keep these with you."

His gaze melted and tears filled his eyes, finally understanding her purpose. "Always."

They were almost late to dinner, as their lovemaking took on an even greater urgency than before. Time had become their enemy now. But Sarah was determined not to be sad until they said their last farewells.

They reached the lobby before Lenore and Gil emerged from the elevator. She and Lenore shared knowing looks when they did. Lenore and Gil had passed the rest of their afternoon the same way.

All of a sudden there was a shout, and two men on the other side of the lobby began fighting. They yelled at the top of their lungs at one another. One was burly, the other slight. But it was the slight one who pushed first. The other pushed back and Sarah nearly fell as the slighter man toppled into her.

"Say 'excuse me'," Mac demanded.

Sarah laid a hand on his arm, but this was not the loving sweet

Mac she knew. This was the First Lieutenant he'd trained to be.

"You nearly knocked my wife off her feet. Say 'excuse me'," Mac growled.

Both men stared then laughed. "In your dreams, kid."

"Apologize."

"Never," the burly man sneered.

For whatever reason, Sarah would never understand, the heavyset man with the attitude charged Mac. One minute he was upright, his fist trying to connect to Mac's jaw, and the next he was face down on the floor, his arm twisted up to his neck and Mac's knee in the center of his back. Then security guards were surrounding them. "Let him go," one ordered.

"Hey," Gil protested, as they grabbed Mac to escort him out of the lobby with the other two. "He didn't start anything."

The security guards didn't seem to care. They took all three men into custody and began heading toward the door next to the front desk, the one marked "Employees Only." Sarah followed, not sure which bothered her more, the elite soldier with the hairpin trigger of a temper, or the realization that they'd probably spend their last night together in jail.

*

Thank God for Lenore and Gil. Gil followed them into the manager's office. He whipped out a card, flashed it at the manager, put it back in the breast pocket of his jacket and said, "You might want to reconsider."

They all stared.

"Gilbert Radovitch, Esquire. I'm acting on behalf of my client, Lieutenant McDonald here. He's a member of the Air Rescue Service. And he just did his job to the fullest extent."

"Excuse me?" the manager said.

"He just saved you from a tremendous lawsuit. If anyone had gotten hurt by this... this gentleman." Gil gave the man a pointed look. "Well, I'm sure that would have been a problem, now wouldn't it?"

"What the fuck are you talkin' about?" the "gentleman" retorted, apparently soused to the gills.

"I object to that kind of language in front of these ladies." Gil's tone matched that of a lawyer taking command of the situation.

Obviously the manager did too. "Get him out of here," he told his assistant. "Put him in your office until I sort this out."

Gil explained the situation, ending with, "As you can see, my client saved you a great deal of trouble and embarrassment. The man is obviously drunk and belligerent. More than ready to cause additional trouble."

The manager nodded and sighed. "I'm sure my client's willing to let it go as long as you are," Gil added.

The man didn't look happy. "Very well."

"And for his time and trouble?" Gil asked with the lift of his brow. "After all, the Lieutenant is on his honeymoon."

Now the manager really looked unhappy. Sarah bit her lip to keep from laughing. The man grimaced as he said, "Of course."

Gil made as if he were thinking, then looked down at his watch. Sarah stared, ready to explode with mirth. Gil lifted his gaze and said, "Dinner on the house will be fine, seeing as how we missed our reservations nearly an hour ago."

"I'll call the restaurant and fix things for you," the man's assistant was quick to reply, earning him a fierce glare from his boss.

"No hard feelings," Mac added. "But I'd keep riff-raff like that out of my hotel if I were you."

Sarah watched everyone shake hands, trying hard to keep silent. She couldn't believe Gil was such an actor. The assistant manager personally escorted them all to the restaurant and waited until they were seated.

"Martinis all the way around," Gil said to the waiter, when the assistant manager finally left.

Lenore reached over and kissed her husband's cheek. "I'm impressed, darling. Maybe we should do it in the afternoon more often."

"Lenore!" Gil erupted, turning beet red.

"Oh for heaven's sake, sweetie. These kids are on their honeymoon. Relax."

Sarah looked at her husband and they both erupted in laughter. "I had no idea you were such an actor," she told Gil as she sobered.

"I didn't either," Lenore chimed in. "Interesting."

Their drinks arrived. "To teaching idiots some manners," Mac said.

"To acting lessons," Gil said.

"To free dinners," Sarah added.

"To sex in the afternoon," Lenore continued, which earned her an elbow to the ribs. "Ow!" And they all laughed again.

Time literally flew by. Sarah explained she was studying at the University of Nevada in Reno, which was near Stead Air Force Base, and Lenore told her she and Gil lived in Reno, a happy coincidence. She and Lenore exchanged telephone numbers then they said good-night. Sarah's eyes filled as she watched Lenore hug Mac and tell him to be careful. Maybe he'd listen to her.

Mac made achingly beautiful love to her, prolonging every moment as if he could stave off the inevitable. Neither of them could. Lying together on their last night, Sarah begged one promise out of him.

"I've been thinking, Mac."

He leaned on his elbow to stare down at her, a sated look on his face. "Yeah?"

"Let's make a promise."

"O... kay," he answered, sounding a bit unsure of what he was getting himself into.

But Sarah knew deep in her heart that she had to do this. "Let's promise to come back here for our first anniversary. To the Excelsior."

He smiled, answering way too quickly. "Okay, sure. Why not?"

"No, Mac. I mean promise. That means you have to live. You have to be here. Same time, same date next year. Do you understand?"

"Look, sweetheart. You know I can't do that. I don't know what's going to happen." When he saw the look on her face, he realized those were the wrong words to use, so he tried to backpedal. "I mean, I don't know where they'll send me. I could end up in New Jersey, for all I know, at the end of my tour."

They both knew she wasn't talking about the end of his tour of duty. "Promise me."

"Sarah…"

"No. I love you. We're going to be here. One year from today. Both of us. You have to promise." Sarah swore she wouldn't, but couldn't help the tears filling her eyes, threatening to overflow.

He sighed. "All right, kitten. Don't cry. I promise. I'll be here."

"And we never say good-bye."

He smiled at Sarah. "And we never say good-bye."

One year later. Excelsior Hotel. Las Vegas.

Sarah remembered every moment, every morsel of her honeymoon.

Oh God, Mac. Where are you?

The pharmacy photos still rested between her fingers and Sarah realized she was bending them. She smoothed the glossy paper with a gentle touch, staring down at the happy faces with envy.

I will not cry.

Thank God for Gil and Lenore. They took her under their wings, watching over her, helping her survive the devastating news that Mac's helicopter went down in a jungle with a name she imprinted in her brain. Đắk Đoa. Đắk Đoa. They called it missing in action. MIA. She called it heart-rending.

He went there to save lives, not give his own.

Sarah reserved the honeymoon suite just as they'd shared. The room hadn't changed. The bed, still cavernous as ever, made her jealous of her memories. Her body ached with need and remembered touches. Vignettes filled her mind. His arms wrapping about her waist. That delectable interlude in the shower.

Sarah rose from the bed. She knew she shouldn't have come. But that was the way with promises.

Gil and Lenore drove her down, deciding they'd had such a good time, they'd come back for another vacation. Sarah knew better but didn't argue. They hovered because they cared. But something inside her wouldn't give up. Mac was still alive. She knew he was.

She used his motto, "That Others May Live" and their promise. If she kept him alive in her heart, if she believed that he'd keep his promise, then she'd keep him alive physically. No matter where he was.

It was as simple as that.

When the room began to close in on her, she went down to the casino and played craps. Just as they had before. Not surprising, she didn't win this time. Walking slowly out of the casino, she saw that Flower Drum Song was still playing. She bought four tickets with the hope that... As she stared at them sitting in her palm, tears threatened and her whole body shook with the need to break down.

Perhaps this wasn't such a good idea after all.

She went back upstairs and ordered room service. She sat in the same chair. Every moment of their laughter played in her heart. But now the food tasted like dust. Only the champagne helped to ease the pain. To us, she toasted silently. Then she downed the contents. Eventually, the glass fell to the carpeting, unnoticed.

When they'd first been together, time had been her enemy for it moved too fast. Time was still her enemy, for now it crawled with the agonizingly slow ticks of a second hand. Finally, she rose, went downstairs, and met Gil and Lenore to watch Flower Drum Song again. Her fist crushed the extra ticket all during the show.

After saying goodnight to her friends, Sarah walked around the hotel a while. She hummed the song, You Are Beautiful, just as she had that night after they'd— This time she didn't hide her tears. She even went to the Tower Bar, but this time the drink tasted lonely. She'd hoped that by recreating their weekend together, she could fill the empty hole inside.

Sadly, it hadn't worked.

Still, she'd promised.

At first she thought she'd be able to sleep in the bed alone. But it was too big, too empty. So she curled up in the loveseat and stared, losing herself in her memories.

She met Gil and Lenore by the pool the next day and they tried to cheer her up. Recounting the story of Gil's one bright moment on stage as he'd played their lawyer, gave her a smile at least. She even walked over to the pharmacy, her fingertips running over the fake paneling of the photo booth, and she remembered every second of them taking the pictures in her hand.

Oh, Mac. I miss you so much.

All of a sudden she realized the Excelsior wasn't a glass slipper any more. Still, she'd promised. She walked back into the lobby, head held high, determined to make Mac proud of her.

The same clerk stood behind the front desk. "Mrs. McDonald?"

Sarah stopped short in surprise. "Yes?"

"Can you come over here please?"

"Of course." Curiosity actually overrode the emptiness for a short moment. "Is something wrong?"

"No, ma'am. I'm sorry if you thought that." He reached under the desk for an envelope. "A gentleman left this for you."

He handed Sarah an envelope, and her brows drew together. Was Gil playing a prank to cheer her up?

She walked through the lobby, opening the envelope. A picture rested inside, and as she turned the envelope upside down, it fell into her palm. Dog-eared, scarred, a bit faded. It was of the two of them. Kissing. It was Mac's.

Her knees buckled. She looked around wildly waiting to see the Air Force Blue uniform and the sergeant who would tell her that her husband was dead. Her throat closed, and she feared she'd never take another breath.

"Sarah?"

She closed her eyes. *Oh God, how could you be so cruel? To give me such a vivid memory at a time like this.*

"Sarah? Kitten?"

Fisting her hands and pressing them against her ears, she shut out the voice. Only then did her nose tell her what her mind was so rudely denying.

That was Mac's cologne.

"We promised we'd never say good-bye. I didn't think that meant we'd never say hello."

Sarah staggered toward him. Her eyelids flew open. "Mac?"

She stared up into a gaze filled with too many emotions. "Oh, Sarah. I'm so sorry."

"You're real?"

He smiled, his gaze flying over her face as if he couldn't believe it either. "Yes, I'm real."

"I don't understand. They told me you were missing four months ago. MIA."

His crown had tarnished. He stood leaning on a cane. New lines and creases had formed in his face that would never go away.

"I was nearly captured. But some villagers helped put my leg together and got me to a company of South Vietnamese soldiers."

A part of him seemed ancient and beyond her care. "The South Vietnamese regulars finally helped me get back to Tan Son Nhut airbase. That took a while. So did my debriefing."

He was alive.

"I asked them not to send word that I'd been found, and begged them to send me instead, since it was getting so close to our anniversary. I'm not sure if was because I was being such a pain or because they were calling me a hero." He grinned. "They finally gave me a medical leave."

She knew he was alive because he'd grinned, and though some of the life had gone out of that devil-may-care curve of his mouth, his dimple was still the same.

"I almost didn't make it in time. We had engine trouble in Okinawa."

Deep inside, her heart told her she could fix that grin. With love.

"Mac," she breathed, running to him and throwing her arms around his shoulders. If she held on long enough, tight enough, he'd never go away again. She finally let go and her palms cupped his cheeks, staring, searching, and daring anyone to tell her it was a dream. "Oh, Mac."

"I love you, Sarah. You kept me alive. I had to get back to you."

He stared down at her, and Sarah knew everything would be all right. He'd heal and they'd mend together.

"How is this possible?" she asked, her mind still in a daze. "I don't understand."

He smiled, love pouring from his gaze. "Of course you do. I promised."

3

SAME TIME, NEXT YEAR

Jeff DePew

1971

In a darkened hotel room, a woman sighed contentedly and snuggled closer to her man, resting her head on his chest. Her hand caressed his muscular stomach, his powerful chest. There were still beads of perspiration from their lovemaking on his skin.

She sighed happily. "I can hear your heart."

He kissed the top of her head, ran his fingers through her thick dark hair. "Yeah? What's it saying?"

She tilted her head to look up at him. She smiled. "It's saying you're in love."

"They say the heart doesn't lie."

"They say?" she teased, "What about you?"

"They're right." He pulled her closer and kissed her deeply on the lips. "You are so beautiful. And I do love you."

They lay like that, bodies entwined, content in both each other and their love. After a few minutes, he wriggled free and reached for his watch on the nightstand.

He glanced at the glowing hands.

"Do you have to go?" She rolled over and lay half on top of him, her chin on his chest. She gazed into his eyes. His beautiful green eyes. She could just make them out in the ambient light coming through the curtains. The neon flash of the Las Vegas Strip, just outside, but in this room, at this moment, so far away.

"No. We have some time." He returned the watch, grabbed a pack of cigarettes from the nightstand, shook two out, put them in his mouth, lit both with a silver lighter and handed her one.

"How was Kat's recital?"

She brightened at the thought of her daughter. "She was so cute. She was the loudest one there. She was practically shouting the song."

He chuckled. "Sorry I missed it. She's such a great kid." He stared into the darkness and exhaled. "I wish I could have been there."

"So do I, sweetheart."

He strolled over, stubbed out his cigarette in the ashtray. "So. Have you talked to Leo?"

No answer.

"I'll take that as a 'no'."

"It—it's not that easy. You don't know Leo. He hates that we're even separated."

"He hates it? He'd rather stay in a rotten marriage?"

Her voice was a whisper. "He says he won't ever let me go."

"So don't ask him. Just leave. Call a lawyer, file for divorce, and stay with me."

"I can't do that. If I leave him, he'll go for full custody of Kat. He's threatened me with that already…"

The man exhaled, reached over and stubbed his cigarette out in an ashtray. He sat up and moved to the edge of the bed. He put his head in his hands. She came up behind him and held him, arms laced around his chest.

"It'll be okay, sweetheart." She kissed his ear, his neck. "I just need a little more time. I'm just waiting for the right time."

"I know, baby. It's just… I'm tired of waiting. I want you all to myself."

He got up and went to the window. Pushed the curtain open, revealing more light. She looked at him silhouetted in the window. His broad shoulders and powerful back and legs. He was such a… a man, she thought. Not like Leo.

He turned and faced her, his emerald eyes glinting in the darkness. "You and Kat should live with me. There's no reason you should stay here. I have plenty of room at my place. You could—"

There was a knocking at the door.

He reached down, found his pants and pulled them on. "Did you order room service?"

The woman slid across the bed, the away from the door. "No. Maybe—"

The knocking intensified. became pounding.

"Son of a bitch!" Angry already, now with someone to take it out on. He headed toward the door, guided by the crack of light beneath. More banging—no, now it was kicking. The door nearly burst off its hinges.

"This better be important!" The man yelled, reaching for the knob. "I don't know who you are, but—"

As he turned the knob, the door splintered open, slamming into the wall. The man stumbled backward, off balance.

A figure, black against the light from the corridor, stood in the doorway. He was holding something in one of his hands. She couldn't tell what it was, but it was shiny. He took a step into the room and raised his arm. An explosion filled her ears. Bright light. Another. She saw her man fall and called out his name. The figure pointed his gun at her. Sound. Light. Pain. And then... darkness.

*

2001

Lanie Hobbes stared across the lobby with a satisfied smile. This was it. Her first shift at the front desk of the Excelsior, one of Las Vegas' most storied and upscale hotels. The high ceilings, the beautiful, ornate chandeliers, the plush, red velvet furniture. Night was falling outside and the lobby was filling up with well-dressed guests and gamblers. A piano tinkled faintly from a nearby cocktail lounge.

Lanie was a little nervous, but she had studied the handbooks, watched carefully during her job shadowing, and asked a ton of questions. Six months of working in banquets dealing with stressed out brides and party planners? This should be a walk in the park. She'd be fine. She looked down at herself, smooth down her red shirt, straightening her name tag.

Lanie was organizing room brochures when she sensed a customer. She brushed a loose strand of dark hair out of her face and smiled prettily at the guest.

"Good afternoon, ma'am, welcome to the Excelsior. How may I help you?"

The woman was older, maybe mid-sixties, but very polished and put-together. Dark hair in a stylish bun, sharp cheekbones, bright blue eyes. A streak of white ran through her hair just above her right ear. It was kind of striking, really. It suited her. Charcoal gray Chanel suit. She smiled back at Lanie.

"My name is Jessica King. I have a reservation."

"Of course. One second." Lanie punched in her passcode and looked up Ms. King's information. While the computer was processing, she tried some small talk. It was important to make the guests feel welcome.

"So is this your first time at the Excelsior, Ms. King?"

Jessica King gave a faint smile. A sad smile, Lanie would later think. "No. I—I have been here many times."

"Wonderful! Glad to have you back!" Lanie beamed. "Well, here's your—" She stopped, looking at her computer monitor. This couldn't be right. "Um…"

Lanie couldn't tear her eyes away from the screen. King, Jessica, Room 732 Blocked. See MOD. What? Room 732? But that room was off limits. They had told her that during her training. Was this a mistake? Lanie looked to her right, but Ed, the other employee, was with a customer. She looked to her left. No one. She was on her own.

"Is something wrong?" Ms. King's voice was soft and controlled.

"No, um, but I think there's an issue with your room. Can I offer you another room?"

"What?" Ms. King seemed stunned. She put a hand on the counter to steady herself. "No. I don't want another room! I always stay there."

Lanie's mind was whirling. On the one hand, there was an unwritten policy not to allow guests to reserve room 732. She didn't know why, and it wasn't in any of the employee manuals. There wasn't a even a key code in the system for room 732. But this woman had clearly reserved room 732 and expected to stay there. *Aggh! What to do?*

"Ms. King! So good to see you again!" A dark shape swooped in beside Lanie, gently, but forcefully nudging her to the side. Mark Younger. The shift manager. Tall, square-jawed, his brown hair cut close. He was very good-looking, very professional… and very gay, Lanie had been told.

"This young lady is saying there's a problem with my room." Ms. King's voice faltered a bit, but she managed to maintain her composure.

Mark glanced at the computer screen, raised his head in a dazzling smile. "No, ma'am. Everything looks fine. Room 732. One night."

Ms. King looked relieved. She straightened up.

Mark turned to Lanie. "Lanie, uhhh... could you please scan and sort the key cards from today's shift? Thanks so much." He turned back to Ms. King. "I do apologize, Ms. King. Lanie has just started here and hasn't been briefed on all our policies."

Sort the key cards? Lanie thought. *What the hell does that mean?* She could swipe them, for sure, to clear the code for the next guest room, but sort them? She walked toward the box containing the cards, puzzled. She turned to ask Mark what he meant, when she saw him reach into his pocket, pull out an actual KEY with a plastic tab on it, which was printed, no doubt, the room number 732, and hand it to Ms. King. Ms. King smiled gratefully, clasped Mark's hands in both of hers.

"Thank you so much," she beamed.

"Will you be dining at one of our restaurants tonight?" Mark smiled. "I'd be happy to make your reservations."

Ms. King seemed to think about it. "No, I think I'll be ordering room service. I'm a bit tired."

Mark nodded. "Of course. Would you like help with your bags?"

She looked down at her small roller suitcase and smiled at him. "No, I think I'll be okay. These little wheelie suitcases are so easy."

Mark watched as, limping slightly, she made her way to the bank of elevators. He smiled patiently, then motioned Lanie back over to him. The smile never left his face as he whispered out of the side of his mouth. "Sorry about that. I was stuck in a meeting and couldn't get down here in time to meet her."

Lanie looked at him, then over at Ms. King, who was standing across the lobby waiting for an elevator. "What was that all about? Count the key cards? *Really?*"

He held out his hands in a placating gesture. "I know, I know. I'm sorry. But, it's a very sensitive issue. Ms. King is a very loyal client. Been coming here for years."

"And she always stays in the same room?"

Mark nodded, looked around, then pulled Lanie into an alcove. "No one else ever uses that room. That's why it's blocked. Only Ms. King stays in room 732."

Lanie looked up at him, clearly confused. "But why? What's the big deal? And was that an actual key you gave her?"

Mark smiled patiently. "I can tell you what I know. If you're working at the front desk, they should have told you anyway. But since they haven't, keep it on the down low."

Lanie nodded. "Sure. of course"

Mark looked around again, leaned close to Lanie. "Didn't you ever hear anything about the murder-suicide back in the seventies?"

Lanie shook her head.

"Well, Ms. King was married at the time, and was having an affair with one of the casino managers. Her husband was Leonard King. Heard of him?"

Again, Lanie shook her head. Mark leaned against the wall and folded his arms.

"Girl, where are you from? You never heard about the Leonard King murder? Anyway, Leo King was a big real estate developer. Some say he was connected. He owned a piece of the hotel too. Anyway, he found them in bed and shot and killed her boyfriend. He shot her. And then he shot himself."

"Here? In the Excelsior?"

"I'll give you one guess which room." Mark smiled sinisterly.

Lanie stared at him, open-mouthed. "No! And she stays there? That is so creepy!"

"I can't argue with that. But it's true. After the murder there was a big lawsuit. I don't know all the details, but she was basically given that room. No one else is allowed to use it as long as she's alive."

"But why would she do that? You'd think she'd want to forget about it."

Mark shrugged and glanced at his watch. "The female mind continues to be a mystery to me, darling. Anyway, we have to get back to work. You can buy me a few cocktails after work and I'll fill you in on all the sordid details." Mark gave her a little wave and headed through a door into the inner workings of the hotel.

Lanie headed back to the front desk, thinking about Ms. King. Why would she keep coming back after all this time? And what did she do up there?

She woke up in an empty hospital room. She was alone and frightened. Her head hurt and she couldn't feel her right leg. It was dark and silent, except for the humming of some machine next to her bed and the occasional voice outside her room. She cried out for help, for someone to help her, and an older nurse had come in and calmed her down. The nurse had sat with her for some time, explaining what had happened. She had been shot twice. One bullet had shattered her right kneecap, and the other had grazed the side of her head. The doctor believed she had suffered a concussion but couldn't be sure without talking to her. She had been unconscious for about twelve hours.

"My daughter? Who has my daughter?"

She was with the housekeeper. She was fine.

"And the man? The man who was—in the room with me? Where is he?"

The nurse had stood and said she didn't know. But her eyes betrayed her. She knew. The nurse had excused herself and had left the room.

Jessica King waited patiently for her elevator. When it arrived, she got in, closely followed by three twenty-somethings in skimpy outfits and dangerously high heels. The trio spent the entire elevator ride riveted to their cell phones, laughing and occasionally nudging one another to share something on their screens. Whatever it was only elicited more laughter. Jessica smiled at them and shook her head. Had she ever been like that? That young and carefree? Well, she had, she supposed, until—the bell dinged, the three girls looked up, and still laughing, spilled out into the fifth floor corridor.

At the seventh floor, Jessica got out, tugged her suitcase over the threshold and turned left. She actually could have used a bellhop to carry her suitcase, but it was always so awkward once they go the room. She tried to tip them at the elevator, but they usually wouldn't hear of it. They always wanted to escort her to her room and show her around. Her? She knew the room better than they ever would. And then when they saw how it was decorated... that always led to questions.

Exactly a year after the shooting, she returned to the room. She wanted to see it one last time. The trial had lasted most of the year. Her lawyers had insisted she sue the hotel. At first she had refused, just wanting the whole terrible incident to go away. Just take care of her hospital bills and rehab and forget about it. But they had told her it was the hotel's responsibility to ensure the safety of all guests, and by allowing one of their owners to shoot two guests, they were not protecting their guests. And she had her daughter to think about. This type of settlement could guarantee her daughter's future. So she had acquiesced.

Kat was with her grandmother for the day. She had not told either one where she was going. They wouldn't understand. And she couldn't blame them. How could she explain wanting to come back here one last time? Except for her time with Kat, this was the only place she had really been happy for the past five years. She wanted to see it one last time. To say goodbye.

She leaned her cane against the wall and fished out the passkey she had been given and opened the door. Because it was a crime scene, and considered evidence, it had not been used since the shooting. The carpet and the door had been replaced, but the furniture was the same. Eventually, they would come in and sanitize it, repaint it and replace the furniture and it would be just like every other room, indistinguishable from the rest. But it wasn't any other room. It was their room.

As soon as she entered the room, she had felt something… familiar and comforting. A feeling of peace spread through her. She was almost at the window, when she realized she wasn't limping. A movement out of the corner of her eye, she turned. She gasped.

She stopped outside room 732 and let go of the suitcase. This was always the hardest part. Would it happen this time? Was it even right that she do this? Should she turn around, taxi to the airport, and head home? And then what? She had her beautiful house overlooking the ocean, she had her friends, and, of course, she had her darling Katherine and the grandkids. Her life was good, she knew, but something was missing. Something she could only find in the Excelsior. So she was here. Again.

She belonged here. This was where she wanted to be.

She took the key from her coat pocket and looked at it. She turned it over in her hands. How many times had she held this key?

She reached forward and unlocked the door.

The room was dark, and although she knew where the light switch was, she didn't hit it. The room had to be dark. Otherwise it wouldn't work.

She pulled her suitcase into the room, shut the door and locked it. Checked the lock.

Jessica walked further into the darkened room. She knew this room intimately. But even without the room lights, she could just make out the shape of the bed from the light coming through the

42

bottom of the door. The nightstand right there, and the dresser near the window.

She shivered and hugged herself. It was cold. But she knew she wouldn't be cold for long. As she continued into the room, her right knee relaxed and her limp disappeared. Her posture improved, and even though she couldn't see it, the white streak in her hair faded away.

"You look more beautiful every time I see you."

A shadow detached itself from the wall beside the window. Green eyes glinted as it moved closer, the outline of a man becoming clearer and more solid. He was here. Her man. After all these years. Even death couldn't keep them apart.

They embraced, and their lips met. They kissed hungrily, passionately. No talking was needed. What was there to say? She held his face in her hands. That face she knew so well. That face that would be forever young; forever hers and hers alone. His hands ran through her hair, now no longer in a bun. He caressed her neck. He kissed her her cheeks, her forehead and her lips. He moved down to kiss her neck, now the smooth neck of a twenty-five year old.

They fell together onto the bed.

*

Hours later they in bed. She rarely slept when she was here; and it wasn't because of the sex. There was plenty of that, to be sure. But just to lie with him and talk; sometimes that was the best part. He asked questions upon questions; about Kat, the grandkids, her house, everything she had been up to since last year. He couldn't hear enough. And she loved to share her life with him.

As dawn approached , he held her close and gazed into her eyes. He was starting to fade as night gave way to morning. This was the hardest part.

"You'll be back?"

She kissed him. "Of course, my darling. Same time, next year."

4

WHAT THE HELL HAPPENED IN VEGAS!

A Pauline Sokol romantic short story

Lori Avocato

I turned around 360 degrees in the lobby of Vegas' Excelsior Hotel and thought it was superb in design and decor, admiring the high-end beauty built back in 1960 by Louis "The Lip" LaFica (I didn't even want to go there!). Marble, gold, every kind of expensive material there was on Earth had been used. Not that I was an expert on expensive. Nope, not me. I struggled for every dollar I earned in a job I hated. But looking at all this beauty didn't hurt my eyes at all, so I kept on gawking like a guy in Victoria's Secret shop. Oh... my... god. I looked from the front desk to the lobby center to the doorway, all of which amazed me more. And then, I froze in place when I noticed... *him*. Not even the magnificence of the place could rival what my glare caught at that moment.

Jagger.

No last name that I was aware of. Just *Jagger*.

In his full glory. Well, maybe not full glory, but definitely full "hotness." Tall, always wearing black, Jagger, now wearing faded jeans (rather snug, *gulp*), camel-colored suede sports jacket and a white shirt. Spotless, I'm sure, white shirt. Dark glasses, not needed in the brilliant lobby, but no doubt adding to the attraction and sensuality walking toward me.

And right *past* me.

Ready to yell out, "What the hell?" I realized this fantasy-land hotel was not Hope Valley, Connecticut where I'd come from. Most of my medical insurance fraud cases were in and around that New England area. But today, Fabio Scarpello, my sleazy boss, had managed to send me to dreamland.

Las Vegas.

Apparently *with* Jagger.

Thank you, Saint Theresa.

I said that speedy little thanks to my favorite saint. Being Catholic, living with a "Catholic School Induced Conscience," I had to give praise where it was due. And, looking at hottie Jagger's butt while he stood at the registration desk (no doubt making all the female clerks, okay, in Vegas maybe even the male clerks swoon), St. Theresa was due my gratitude. Jagger and I had done well on all our cases, in the beginning mostly due to his experience, but I had come a long way if I had to say so myself. Being a nurse, I had good instincts, and it turned out I even surprised myself on some cases.

Probably surprised Jagger too, although he'd never admit it.

And, I'd gotten pretty damn street-smart in the process. Coming from a good Polish Catholic family, it took some time to grow in this field, but due to financial need (never, I repeat, never co-sign a loan for a "friend"), and the help of my dear roommates/now legal spouses Miles and Goldie, I began doing damn well with this medical insurance fraud stuff. Miles was a nurse too, darling friend, and when I burned out of the field of nursing he found me investigative work with Fabio. Goldie, ex-Army Intel, was my "mentor" in the beginning as he, too, worked for Fabio. But Goldie also taught me how to dress and do my makeup. He was as chic as they came, as sophisticated as a royal, and as fashion savvy as Coco Chanel, who Goldie once told me had said, "In order to be irreplaceable, one must always be different." And, since Goldie usually looked more like Donatella Versace than her late brother Gianni, he followed Chanel's advice to a "T."

I hurried toward the front desk to make sure cheap Fabio hadn't booked only one room for Jagger and me—then I slowed. Would that really be so bad?

Jagger stood leaning on the desk in the most casual, sexy pose as I approached. Damn. As usual, he always smelled delicious. Manly. But not like Irish Spring soap. Nope. Much more viscerally male. I convinced myself that he had a custom made cologne, or, anything he wore was enhanced by his male pheromones, so he always smelled delicious.

"Yes, Sir," the poor clerk mumbled and couldn't take her eyes off of him while she finished with, "Your room is on the seventh… no, ninth floor and has a lovely view of the Strip. Since we are pretty much centered in the middle of the Strop… Strip. We're in the middle. Centered. Of the Strip." Then she cleared her throat.

Poor kid.

I knew that clearing her throat wouldn't empty the Jagger-induced sexual cobwebs from her mind. Sometimes it took me hours. Ok, days.

"Excuse me." I tried to lean over as Jagger had been doing, but at over six feet he was much taller and my arm slid off the counter top, and I fell against him. *Oops. Gulp. Yum.*

"Easy, Sherlock," he said, while still looking at the doe-eyed clerk, and with his right arm, kinda nudged me upright.

I felt my face burning. And here I thought nothing he could do would still affect me. Ha! Even I didn't buy that one. "Pauline," I corrected (however, in all honesty, I loved that he'd given me a nickname even if it was originally probably an insult to my lack of ability. After a time, I managed to convince myself that wasn't true, and loved that he called me Sherlock. Often I would "guide" my thoughts about Jagger to my own liking.

The clerk handed Jagger two room keys, which he stuck in his pocket. Two?

I held the counter for support and said, "Excuse me. I'm Pauline Sokol. I need to check in too."

While the clerk seemed to ignore me, Jagger took my arm. "You are." He then turned and started to walk toward the elevator after picking up his carry on black leather bag. Black, of course. Not on wheels, of course.

Knowing this kind of Jagger stuff caused my mouth to drop, I shut my lips tightly, yanked on my roll-on bag and hurried behind him. That's right. He had two keys. Nice of him to take care of registering me too. "Is my room on the same floor? With the lovely view? In the center of the Strip?" I shut up since even I thought I sounded like the poor clerk.

Jagger continued on, pressing the "Up" button on the elevator.

I inhaled his scent, the door opened, he stepped in and looked at me frozen on the spot. Being in such close quarters with him never had a good outcome. "I'll wait for the next one." I knew how stupid that was because the damn elevator was empty except for him.

He shrugged, reached into his pocket while he held the door open with his foot (wearing his usual black leather boots) and pulled out one of the keys.

As I reached to take it, he moved his foot, the door started to close, and I grabbed the key before it fell down the tiny crack leading to the elevator shaft.

Shaft.

Oh... my... god. Good thing I waited and didn't get in with him.

*

I accidently pushed the button to floor seven, cursed the foolish clerk, and hit the button for nine. Luckily Jagger had given me the key with the holder, so my room number was on it. Then again, this was Jagger I was talking about. He could think of what to do in a split second and always be right. When the door opened, I stepped out and followed the directions on the wall and found my room, stuck the key in, pulled it out quickly and pushed down on the handle when the light turned green. So far so good. Being flustered by Jagger seemed to be subsiding quickly. I opened the door, held it with my hip, yanked my suitcase through and stopped.

"What took you so long, Sherlock?"

I should have thought, *why am I not surprised?* But nothing about being with Jagger, working with Jagger, or spending hours staring at Jagger, even phased me now. "Took the scenic route. This place is amazing." I looked around the room. Lots of black, white and, well, monochromatic black and white. Interesting. I'd read up on The Excelsior Hotel before coming here, so I knew there was no particular theme or design. But this room screamed male. Male.

Jagger, now lounged out on the king-sized bed with chrome headboard, three steps to get up to it and, oh… my… god, a mirror above. How very Vegas. His shirt was undone in front—all the way down, no shoes or socks on his feet and his hair a bit tousled, but nonetheless, delicious still. I reigned back my Jagger thoughts (as those damn things never worked out well for me either like the close quarters issues) and looked around the room.

Windows overlooked the strip. The floor was some kind of white marble, I was guessing material, and the furniture expensive black and white leather. I let go of my suitcase handle and touched the top of a very comfortable looking white stuffed chair. "Butter," I mumbled.

Jagger raised an eyebrow.

"Ok, I'm not used to such opulence. You sure Fabio only booked one room?" Great. I can't believe I said that. I would have to be a big girl about this and try to control my Jagger-induced lust. That would not be simple. He wasn't just easy on the eyes, but a great guy too. Each year he came to my parents' 1960s nostalgic house for Christmas Eve and a few other times where he'd won the heart of one Stella Sokol, a.k.a Mom. And that was no easy feat. She was super straight, very Polish-traditional and had raised five kids by instilling a conscience in us along with the help of the nuns at the Catholic school we had all attended. She called him "Mr. Jagger." *Geez.* But to his credit, he never corrected her. How cute was that?

Plus, I shared a joint Shih Tzu/poodle mix with Goldie and Miles. Although the poor thing only weighed in at nine pounds, Spanky was a great judge of character. And, he loved Jagger. Good enough for me.

"Take a look at this," I heard him say, and before I could swing around, I thought, at what? He was on the bed, for crying out loud. His shirt was undone, for crying out loud and his feet naked.

I heard a shuffling sound and, although my mind wanted to wander into the "taking-off-clothing" arena, logically it sounded like paper. Sure enough. I turned to see the stereotypical manila case file folder on the bed next to him. True Fabio form: a used folder.

Right. We were here to work. I cursed cheap Fabio for only coughing up enough for one room, and walked toward the bed. "I'll unpack later." I picked up the file. "What do we have here?"

49

I think Jagger shifted toward me, but I focused on the folder. "Chiropractor fraud."

"Chiropractor? This is the land of casinos and shows? Who goes to a chiropractor here?"

He gave me a kinda, "read the file" look but said, "High rollers."

"High rollers as in gamblers?"

He nodded.

"But that doesn't sound illegal. The casino provides a massage or two to people who spend a lot of money?"

"Chiropractor. Not masseuse. Read the file, Sherlock." With that, he was up off the bed, down the steps and headed toward the bathroom. "Order me a ribeye, rare, salad without dressing, and something for yourself. Could be a long night." He took his suitcase with him, so I guessed he was going to change. Get comfortable.

Oh geez. Comfortable.

"Where should I go to get…" He'd closed the door. I stared at it a few minutes as if it could answer me, then realized how very small-town-America I sounded. Room service. Never in my life had I ever used expensive room service. I only hoped Fabio had given us a daily spending allowance to cover it. Deciding to investigate the room before studying the file, I found the menu, the phone, a small refrigerator stocked with snacks, liquor, beer and soft drinks. This *was* the Disneyland of hotels.

Room service took my order for Jagger's steak and my alarmingly expensive burger. I unpacked so my clothes would unwrinkle and sat on a black couch which overlooked the Strip. Even in the daylight, the place sparkled. I opened the file folder and started to read. Apparently the casino provided services from this chiropractor gratis for people who spent a lot of money gambling. Still, I didn't see what the guy was doing that was so wrong. I kept reading then felt something next to me.

Shoeless Jagger had sat down next to me. And he must have showered, because his hair was still a bit wet. Wet. He still smelled freshly delicious, and now wearing faded jeans and a black (naturally) T-shirt, he looked over my shoulder.

Help me, Saint Theresa.

How the hell could I concentrate like this? What was Fabio thinking? Maybe he did this on purpose, as he'd never been too fond of me, but I was the medical expert and our cases always were medical insurance fraud. Wait. I was being silly. Fabio had no idea about my Jagger-infatuation. Only Goldie and Miles knew. I had to be professional, so I managed to say, "I don't see the fraud aspect yet."

As Jagger started to say something, a doorbell rang. A doorbell? In a hotel? He got up, went to answer it, and when he stepped aside, a waiter rolled in a lovely silver cart, and the aroma of steak and my twenty-two dollar burger wafted throughout the room.

*

The meal was delicious, and watching Jagger chow down on a rare ribeye was even more appetizing. Soon, we had cleaned our plates. He rolled the cart toward the door and stuck it outside the room. He'd signed the check on it earlier, and I'm sure he'd given the guy who delivered it a good tip.

"Ok," Jagger said, taking the file from the coffee table. "They provide this service, but somewhere along the line, the insurance company is getting hosed. We have to figure out how. Use your medical expertise."

"Um." I needed more to go on. "What's this guy's deal? Does it say what he does?"

"She."

She? *She*? All I could think was: *hope she is not a looker!*

"So Fabio gave us some chips…"

Jagger was still talking, but I'd zoned out on the "she" part. I pulled myself together and looked at him. "Chips?" Why would Fabio give us potato… ah, *gambling chips*. I laughed. "Oh. I get it. Hope he doesn't expect me to be using the damn chips."

He looked at me as if to say, "Duh." But he rifled through the folder while mumbling, "I got that one."

Phew. "So what is my job then? Besides the medical part."

Just as Jagger rearranged the folder, the doorbell rang again.

"Did you order more room service?" I got up, since he didn't look too keen on moving, and headed to the door. "I don't have any cash to tip—" I said, yanking the door open.

"Hello, Suga'!"

"Oh my gosh! Goldie. Goldie? What are you doing here?"

"Can I come in to explain?" He'd worn his royal blue suit with

51

the pencil skirt, heels that matched perfect in color and had to be a gazillion inches high, and a white fur boa, even though it had to be eighty degrees outside. A curly, down to his shoulders blond wig added to chic. Still, Goldie never looked overdressed.

Jagger yelled, "Let him in, Sherlock, and close the door."

Right. We were doing detective work, so we had to be careful no one got suspicious of us. Never knew who was lurking in a classy hotel like this in Vegas. However, six-foot Goldie in drag never looked suspicious.

"Come in," I said, grabbing his arm and yanking him and his Louis Vuitton luggage in the door, then closing it. I hugged him again. Goldie was always my "ally" in fraud cases and in love (Ok, and in Jagger fantasies). I looked at his three bags. Even for Goldie this was excessive. "Why so much luggage? How long you staying?" Was he bunking with us? *Yay. Or damn.*

Goldie looked at Jagger. "Hey." Then he turned toward me. "Guess he didn't get to tell you yet."

Did Jagger snicker? I looked at him, since he had made some kind of noise, and in my past experiences with him, the noise was usually derogatory toward me. But not in a mean way. "What?"

Jagger got up, shook Goldie's hand, said, "Drink?" and headed to the refrigerator.

Goldie flopped down on the white leather chaise lounge, which only added to the beauty of his outfit, matching perfectly, and said, "Champagne." Then he flicked one size eleven heel onto the floor, followed by the other in an oh-so-ladylike style.

Oh how Goldie. "I'll join him," I said and snuggled up next to Goldie.

Jagger took out a bottle of Dom Perignon, which was very expensive stuff. He popped the cork, poured a lovely crystal glassful for Goldie, used the same kind of fancy glass for me and got himself a Heineken—without a glass.

I kissed Goldie's cheek while Jagger said, "He's here for you, Sherlock."

Did Fabio (or more likely Jagger) think I wasn't capable of working this case? *Shoot.* "Wait a damn minute. I have the medical knowledge—"

"Relax, Sherlock. You got that. We know it." Jagger took a long swig of his beer. "That's not what I meant."

Goldie turned toward me with a kinda pathetic look on his face, meaning I looked pathetic, not him. "What he means is, I am here to dress you!" He laughed and said, "This is going to be so much fun! I'm gonna make you look like a star. A rich-ass star. Maybe royalty. Yes, foreign royalty! Princess Sokol!" With that, he set his champagne down on the glass and chrome coffee table and headed toward one of the Louis', the smallest one like a makeup case. "I brought everything I need, Suga'. Makeup. Shoes. Clothes!" He unzipped one of the bags and eased out a sparkling number in black. "*Magnifique!*"

Before I could remind myself that Goldie grew up in the French Quarter of New Orleans, I realized the gown was not only sparkly, but *sheer*. I sneaked a peek at Jagger, who seemed to be grinning, although his lips hadn't moved. Oh, how very Jagger.

"It's lovely, Goldie, but I'm still confused. Why would I need such fancy clothing when I'm here to investigate fraud? I mean, I thought we'd be doing most of our work in the dead of night, wearing black, but not sparkly, sexy black. I'm thinking T-shirt, black. Maybe a hoodie."

Jagger was the master of disguise in this partnership. Once he managed to fool me (ok, he fooled me a lot) with a senior citizen getup. Even then, he looked delectably hot. And I had started to tell myself that age really didn't matter.

Goldie looked at Jagger and raised an eyebrow. "You really didn't tell her yet?"

It wasn't a question. More an accusation. Atta boy, Goldie. You've got my back.

Jagger took longer swigs of beer, all the while looking at me over the rim of the bottle. When he swallowed, he said, "I told you, he is a *she*. Dr. Genevieve Pardue. I'll use the chips, you distract the crowd."

I nearly spit out my sip of champagne, when I realized Jagger was saying I was capable of distracting the crowd—the crowd of mostly men, I guessed. Then again, when Goldie got done with me, that was entirely possible.

But wait. Did that mean *Jagger'd* be distracting Dr. Pardue?

*

"Close your lids, Suga'." Goldie held my head back with one hand while he applied more mascara to both eyelashes.

"Feels like enough. I don't think I can open my eyelids with all that gunk on them. Way too heavy already."

Goldie chuckled. "Hold on." He rubbed something very gently over my eyelids. "Flecks of black and gold. Marvelous."

Even though my eyes were closed, I inhaled Jagger and heard him say, "Let him do his job, Sherlock."

"I—" My eyelids opened.

Goldie intervened with, "You sit." He pointed to Jagger. "You," He took my arm. "Come with me."

I followed him into the gigantic bathroom. All I could think was that Stella Sokol would go through a bottle of Windex with all the mirrors in this place. Who really wanted to see themselves naked in the wall to wall mirrors? Then she'd spray a few cans of her famous pine-scented Renuzit, which she loved and was the aroma of my childhood. Along with Polish cooking.

Goldie pulled and prodded as he slid the gown over my body. I'd been a jogger, so at least I'd kept myself in decent shape. But when he zipped up the back, I said, "Holy moley, Goldie, that is tight!"

He looked back, held a finger to his lips and said, "Yes, Suga', indeed it is. You look stunning!"

The last time I saw this dress, Goldie was sliding it out of the makeup-sized suitcase, and that's when I saw the sparkle and the sheer. The sheer is what concerned me. "I'm afraid to look."

He gently took my arm and turned me to the largest mirror in the bathroom. "Look."

"Oh shoot!" The gown came down to the floor on one side and several inches above on the other side, where my leg stuck out. Actually, it looked long and slender. Nice. Good thing I took after my mother as far as legs went. She always used to brag that Sokol women had lovely legs. The heels he'd given me, black, high, strappy ones, helped. The sheer part of the dress ran from mid-waist to the entire bodice, with strategically placed sparkles covering part of my chest. Only part. "I feel like one of the showgirls, Goldie. I can't go out like this!"

He patted my arm. "You are supposed to be Jagger's lover... in a very classy way." He looked at me from head to toe and said, "You fit the bill perfectly."

I wanted to shout, *lover*? But instead I pulled at the dress, which wasn't such a good idea. I looked in the mirror to see my left nipple through the sheer black.

Goldie glared at me and tapped a nail to his teeth. "I don't think you want to touch perfection. Leave it to me and leave *it* the hell alone!"

I agreed. He curled and fluffed my hair and mumbled something about how blond I was, and that, thank goodness, he knew how to do makeup on porcelain skin. "You look more alive." He held out an amazing little clutch of black diamonds, fake I'm sure, but they fooled me.

I smiled and blew him a kiss. "Thanks, Goldie."

He nodded, opened the door and ushered me through.

Jagger, dressed in a tuxedo—black, of course—hair done to look oh-so-delectable and shoes this time, not boots. Black dress shoes. I could almost see my reflection in the shine. He looked like a billion dollars in *this* economy. *Yum.*

He gave me the once over, and while holding back on covering my important parts, I stood graciously tall (even though I wasn't, but the heels helped) and felt rather regal. Thank you, Goldie. I turned to see he had disappeared along with the other two Louis Vs, which I'm sure housed his clothing.

"Meet me in the lobby by the fountain in ten. I have some prep work to do."

I watched Jagger walk toward the door, clicking his heels on the marble floor with each step. Sigh. Prep work? I hope that didn't include the doc!

*

Feeling a bit lost, I took the elevator down to the lobby, figuring I might as well wait there for Jagger. When the door opened, I gasped at the beauty of the place. Marble everything, lots of gold, lots of fancy furniture, and lots of fancy people. The Excelsior was not for the faint of wallet. That'd be me if I wasn't on a case with Fabio footing the bill. I bet he had the insurance company cough up the big bucks in advance. That would be oh so Fabio.

A smartly dressed man in a black uniform came forward. It was then I remembered the "sheer" and tried to cover up. However, I swore to myself I wouldn't touch the damn dress, or I may have another "chic dress malfunction." Guess Goldie knew what he was doing, since lots of heads turned toward me. *Me.*

"May I call you a town car, *mademoiselle?* he asked.

Ready to say you can call me a Volkswagen if you want, I realized he thought I was going out. "No. Thank you, anyway. I'm waiting for someone."

I think he winked at me, or at least my imagination thought so. Nodding at him, I turned and walked toward the gigantic, silken, round seat in the center of the lobby, surrounding the fountain. I sat myself down and enjoyed gawking as I waited for Jagger. A few times I had to shut my lips tightly as several celebrities came and went. Yikes. This has to be the best case I'd ever been on! It sure was the classiest place I'd ever worked.

After what seemed like more than "ten," I noticed the elevator door open and out stepped a few hunks all dolled up in tuxedos. And then *my* hunk followed. *My hunk?* This place was wreaking havoc with my normally intelligent mind.

"Ready, Pauline?" He held a hand out toward me.

That had to be for show, but I took it and quietly said, "I would be, if I knew what the hell I was doing."

He shook his head, a common behavior when we were together. More loudly than he needed, he said, "I've booked us a seat at the baccarat table, darling."

The *baccawhat?* But I knew not to ask, so I took his hand (be still my heart!) and followed him to the elevator. Once inside, he pushed the button for the floor that said, "Casino." I leaned forward and said, "I don't know how to gamble."

"Relax, you aren't going to. Remember?"

Oh, right. I was going to distract the others, if possible. Thank you, Goldie for showing so much of my skin. Before the door opened, I allowed myself to look at Jagger in such close quarters (although the elevators in this place were the size of my condo living room back home) and noticed he'd added a white silk scarf to his outfit.

"Very James Bond," came out of my mouth.

Jagger shook his head again, put his hand against the small of my back and gently ushered me out the door. Luckily, I didn't swoon, whatever that meant.

The casino was more fabulous than the lobby, if that were

possible. Sounds of machines ringing, people's mumbled voices, and an atmosphere of risk all caught my attention. I was about ready to ask Jagger if I could throw a twenty into a slot machine called *Panda Bears*, 'cuz they were so cute, then realized, I'd be throwing the money to Louis the Lip's heirs. And they probably did all right by owning this place, and I could use the twenty more than them.

Jagger led me toward a beautiful set of mahogany doors with stained glass panels. He leaned forward, put his index finger on some kind of pad on the doorframe, then pressed the doorbell.

Doorbell in a casino! I wasn't even going to ask.

Both doors opened simultaneously. A woman in a butler uniform but with cleavage—lots of cleavage—stood at the ready. "Hello, sir," she said, and nodded at Jagger.

Me, she ignored.

"Right this way."

We followed her, and I couldn't help but notice how tightly the pants hugged her butt. And I'm sure Jagger didn't miss it, either. Nothing got past Jagger.

I realized the room was silent. There was a large table in the center. Mahogany, again, but a much deeper reddish shade. Chairs the size of the Queen's throne, but covered in a silken red fabric sat around it. Despite the dark furniture, the room was aglow with crystal chandeliers and sconces shining all around. This was all so cool, I thought, and Jagger held my chair out for me, so I sat without making a fuss. I sure was glad that I wasn't going to have to play.

The others at the table were all dolled up in gowns and tuxedos, looking like they could buy and sell me. Most of the men were playing, and the women there for show. Like me. Ha. The jewels on the ladies did not look like cubic zirconium to me, but my bag and dress could rival their outfits thanks to Goldie.

Soon Jagger had a stack of chips in front of him of various colors that he put into piles. As far as I could see, the denominations were from $100 black to $1000 yellow. Fabio would be having a heart attack right about now. A male waiter came and asked what we would like to drink.

I started to say, "Coors," but was stopped with a Jagger-look, when he said, "The lady will have a martini, dry, and I will have Glenlivet, neat."

I knew that to be an expensive scotch, but was more concerned with how "The Lady" was going to function after a dry or wet martini. Suddenly, several customers turned toward the door, and I was among them. Across from me, a handsome blond guy nearly gave himself whiplash.

In walked a lovely, gorgeous, chic brunette dressed in a white silken pants suit, with her hair curling over her chest, but not enough to cover the excessive cleavage of her tanned skin. I wondered how she could manage to move without a hitch on those white spiked heels. Guess Goldie would do the same, but with more grace, I thought. All the staff nodded to her as she kinda floated across the room. At least in my mind she floated, and I'm sure in every male's mind too. Luckily, Jagger was looking at his cards. Not just looking, but bending them as if to peek at what they were. Almost bending them in half.

Leaning very close, I frantically asked, "What are you doing?" Too close, because I inhaled his delicious fragrance and nearly forgot what I'd asked.

He touched my face, almost sensually, but sadly, I'm sure it was all part of the act. Nope, I was going with sensually for my own benefit. "Relax, darling. It is customary."

I turned to look over my shoulder, to realize he was talking to me. But just as I did, a male butler-type held out the chair next to Jagger—and the woman in white slithered into it!

Great. I felt rather frumpy in my chic outfit and noticed how everyone stared at her, and she seemed to fit right in as if she lived here. I hoped she wasn't one of Louis's heirs!

The dealer leaned toward her and said, "Good day, Doctor Pardue."

Jagger never even broke character, while I just about fell out of my gigantic queen's throne.

Doctor Genevieve Pardue, fraud committing chiropractor, leaned over to Jagger and whispered something.

Damn. She had to be part of the "thing he had to take care of" earlier. And the damn white scarf would have gone perfectly with her outfit. Or was that "from her outfit." Either way, it could strangle her pretty damn good if need be.

*

After what seemed like hours to me, and several lady-like sips of my martini, a smartly dressed man came up to the doc. She nodded, took her chips with her and left.

Thankful, yet not thankful, because now our suspect was gone, I looked at Jagger. "Now what, darling?" Damn that felt good.

"Relax, Sherlock." He pushed a stack of the white $500 chips toward a section of the table marked "Dealer" and took a long, slow sip of his second scotch.

At first, I wondered if the alcohol would cloud his judgement, then I reminded myself this was Jagger. Nothing ever phases him. And the only clouded mind between the two of us was mine.

Jagger pushed another stack of chips forward onto the same spot on the table. In a few minutes, the dealer was pushing an ever larger stack of chips toward Jagger, who didn't blink an eye.

Damn, the guy was good.

I was halfway through my drink when the same smartly dressed man, who'd ushered out the doc, came up and whispered to Jagger, who then collected all of his chips and stood. The man took the back of my chair, so I got up and followed them. If I thought the damn heels made me wobbly, the martini wasn't helping. However, I was a professional, so I made my feet work and cleared my mind as best I could.

Before I knew it, we were in a lovely waiting room decorated in golds and silvers with overstuffed navy leather furniture. Not just any waiting room. The butler-guy had to unlock the unlabeled door for us to get in. Interesting.

I leaned to Jagger. "What are we doing here? It looks like a doctor's—" Duh. "Ok. I get it. Who is she going to treat?" *Me. Please.* Because I sure as hell didn't want her pulling and manipulating anything on Jagger.

He was perfect the way he was.

A door to the left opened, the blond man, who I had noticed in the casino and apparently did give himself whiplash, came out, while saying, "Thanks, Doctor, I feel much better." He rubbed his neck, but I wondered if that was really what she had treated.

Doctor Pardue came forward toward Jagger. "You may come through now."

I got up, and she gave me a look that said sit down. Bitch. He's mine now. But I said, "Darling, do you want me to come in?"

59

Jagger looked at me, then at the reception desk, and I realized what my job was. While he was being "treated" by the gorgeous doc, I was doing the snooping. Thank you very much, Fabio.

"I'll be fine," he said, leaned over and kissed my lips.

My lips. I may not be able to concentrate. I watched him go, looked to see there was no one at the reception desk, and apparently the door was locked to anyone coming in, other than the butler-guy bringing another client. But with this kind of deal, I figured only one person at a time was brought in. What a perk for high rollers. A chiropractic treatment for sore necks or backs when they sat too long looking at their cards and winning a gazillion dollars or losing two.

More determined to get something on this woman, because medical insurance fraud led to higher premiums for the average Joe (and the fact that she was a damn looker now touching Jagger), I went to the reception desk. Slowly, I looked behind it to see if anyone was there. The wall was solid, so no back entryway. The unattended desk was just asking for me to investigate.

I took out my iPhone from the little black bag of fake diamonds that Goldie had fixed me up with, and walked around the desk. I looked up to see a camera on the corner of the ceiling and took a manila folder from the In Box, folded it in half, flipped off my heels and stood on the rolling chair to cover the camera. I managed to do it like a pro and got down safely, then started to snoop before Jagger was done. Done is right. Plus, some security guard was probably fiddling with the monitor for this place when it went black.

Several drawers were unlocked, but nothing of interest stuck out. Behind the desk was a file cabinet. Locked. Shoot. I rifled through the top drawer of the desk where I found a set of keys. Who would be stupid enough to leave the key in the desk, but then this wasn't a permanent doctor's office, so any help might not be too professional or bright. I had read in the file that Doctor Pardue had a practice in a business complex outside of Vegas. This gig here was pretty profitable according to the insurance losses, but not exactly medically professional.

After trying several keys, the lock clicked. I opened the file and pulled out a stack of bills. Bingo. Insurance bills. Without hesitating, I pulled the file of the top few patient's bills to match them to the files on the shelves behind. I studied a few for a minute or two. The diagnoses did not fit the bill. Exaggerated treatment reports, unnecessary chiropractic services that didn't match the CAT scan or MRI reports, and several referrals to one other than Doctor Pardue's practice for continued treatment did stand out. My father used to say, "They get you on the payroll and never let you off." Apparently Stanley Sokol was right in this doc's case. I took pictures of the files and bills with my iPhone. Then, I put everything back, stood on the chair to grab the folder from the camera before a guard came in, grabbed my shoes and hurried to my seat. Just as I collapsed into it, the door opened.

A guard came in, ignored me and looked at the reception desk and ceiling camera. Then, he turned and walked back out. *Phew.* Guess he was one of the not-so-bright employees here.

The Doc's door opened; they both came out, and Jagger looked at me with a question, wondering if I'd ever left my seat.

I held my head up high, tried to stand taller when I got up, then realized my shoes were still off so height wasn't mine this time. At least I'd had the good sense to take my shoes back to the chair. "I need to get back and soak in a long, hot whirlpool, darling. My feet are so sore."

Both Jagger and the doctor stared at me, but I kept on as I headed to the door. "Thank you for taking care of him. I'm sure this place keeps you quite busy," I said as I grabbed Jagger's arm (maybe a little too possessively) and walked him to the door with me. *Me.*

Once outside, I let go, but he took my arm and led me to the elevator. Inside, he looked at me. I hoped he was going to kiss me but didn't allow the magic of Vegas to confuse my thoughts. Soon it would be back to the reality of Hope Valley, Connecticut, working more fraud cases and, sniff, being partners in work only. We had the redeye back to Hartford tonight. The glamour, glitz and pretending in my mind that I was really here *with* Jagger would soon come to a screeching halt.

"So?" Jagger asked.

"Hm?" I looked at him. "Oh, right. Yes, I have photos showing her overcharging, providing unnecessary services and even recommending continued therapy with her. Not much on the bills matched the medical reports."

Jagger didn't flinch. He took me by the shoulders, and I said a quick Saint Theresa prayer that the elevator would get stuck between floors, although I was a bit claustrophobic, and he looked me in the eye. "Atta girl, Sherlock."

The door opened and my knees just about gave out. Those words from Jagger were like an Oscar to a movie star. We headed down the hallway and into our lavish room for the last time. I realized that we weren't even spending the night together, since the case was done. *Damn.* I'd have to be satisfied with our shoulders touching on the plane with every bout of turbulence. I'd find a way to make that sensual for sure.

"You email the pictures to Fabio?"

"Oh, not yet." I slipped off my shoes and sat on the edge of the bed. "Good idea. I'll do that right now. Then he can contact the police." But before I could open the file, I felt him next to me, he eased my phone out of my hand and lifted me up to stand. "What..."

"Shut up, Sherlock," he mumbled and leaned forward.

It was not my imagination this time. Jagger's kiss was real. *Real.*

And what was going to follow was more than real. *Unreal* in my Jagger/Pauline book...

5

KISS ME AND KILL ME WITH LOVE

Connie Corcoran Wilson

Phyllis walked to the radio. She cranked the volume. *The Theme from a Summer Place* filled the large suite at the Excelsior Hotel. Percy Faith's Orchestra engulfed the room with lush strings, the melody repeating the refrain from the 1959 Troy Donahue/Sandra Dee hit film.

It was May of 1960, but the theme from the summer movie was still playing on every radio station in America. The hypnotically romantic melody reverberated in your head. Once heard, it was difficult to get it *out* of your head.

Dorothy, the second oldest of the three McGuire sisters, yelled from the next room at her youngest sibling, "Phyllis, turn that down. You'll wake the dead. It's giving me a headache. I'm trying to think. We have to perform tonight, you know. And tonight is only three hours away."

"Dorothy, you're *in* this movie," twenty-nine-year-old sister

Phyllis replied, with an impish smile. "You ought to be the one turning *up* the volume."

Thirty-two-year-old Dorothy looked peeved.

"I hate that. You *know* I hate that. It's bad enough that we're always being told we copied the Andrews Sisters. Why couldn't the other Dorothy McGuire at least change her last name when she started acting? Sylvia Hunter. That's her character name in the movie. Maybe use 'Hunter' to keep us separate. Or use her maiden name." Dorothy scowled.

The sisters had had this conversation before, when the movie premiered. The singer named Dorothy McGuire also disapproved of the movie's plot. Two married people in unhappy marriages (one of them played by the actress Dorothy McGuire) start an affair after many years apart, while their teen-aged children (Dee and Donohue) fall in love at first sight.

"I didn't approve of that movie. All that premarital and extramarital sex. Doris Day had it right. Don't promise what you aren't going to deliver. Dorothy McGuire may be a good actress, but Sylvia Hunter was a bad wife. It's not the way we did things back in Ohio. It's not the way Mom raised us in Middletown." Dorothy shot a knowing glance at her youngest sister, who remained blissfully indifferent to Dorothy's disapproval. Tacit criticism of Phyllis' wilder lifestyle.

"Oh, come on! Don't go all virtuous on me. Sandra Dee and Troy Donohue were magic together, and Lord knows the Sylvia character deserved to have a little fun with her old flame. Her husband in the film was a drunk. Lighten up, Dorothy! You're beginning to sound like Mom. You're becoming old before your time." Phyllis smiled.

"Someone has to keep you two on the straight and narrow," said Dorothy. Dorothy was only half-kidding. She *was* the oldest in attitude. Christine might be technically the oldest of the three, but Dorothy was the one enforcing rules and calling rehearsals. Dorothy felt the burden of setting a good example for her sisters, dispensing advice when necessary. Lately, it was more needed than earlier in their careers, which, in Phyllis' case, began when she was only four years old. Phyllis had now been singing with her two sisters, Dorothy and Christine, for a quarter of a century.

"Dorothy, you worry too much. This Dorothy McGuire is a fine actress. She was great in *Old Yeller*." A smile played around the edges of Phyllis' lips. She was egging her older sister on. It was what Phyllis did. She liked to get things going. Have fun. Be the center of the action. Be in the know. It was why Phyllis liked show business so much and wasn't at all interested in settling down.

Dorothy and Christine both had boyfriends. Dorothy wasn't married yet, however, and her steady was back home in Ohio. She still could enjoy the attention of a handsome suitor. The difference was that Dorothy was more cautious about who she went out with than Phyllis was.

Phyllis didn't have the time or the inclination to think about settling down. Why worry, when there were so many fish in the sea? Her dance card was full. That was the way Phyllis liked it. As she often pointed out to her sisters when they tried to give her unsolicited advice, "I'm not even thirty yet. Give me a break!"

What Phyllis didn't like was the feeling that her older sisters were always trying to rein her in, trying to impose their moral code on her. Phyllis' own motto was *live and let live*. If asked, she might have added, *You're only young once*.

Dorothy responded with sarcasm at the reference to the 1957 tear-jerker about a dog. Dorothy said, "Maybe she should have kept her original maiden name, so people wouldn't confuse us."

Phyllis said, "Not likely. Her maiden name was Hackett." Both women giggled at Phyllis' mention of the Omaha-born actress' unpleasant-sounding real last name.

Dorothy smiled. Learning this, she said, "Then again, maybe not." Both sisters laughed.

The conversation turned to that night's performance.

The McGuire Sisters were opening for Johnny Carson.

Carson was the daytime host of *Who Do You Trust?* His television pilot, *Johnny Come Lately*, was under consideration by the networks. When Carson, Red Skelton's head writer, filled in for an injured Skelton on Skelton's television show on KNXT in 1954 (Red knocked himself out one hour before airtime), Johnny's monologue went well, giving the Corning, Iowa, native his big break.

Louis 'The Lip' LaFica, the Excelsior's owner, thought Carson was going places. He booked Carson in the Excelsior's main ballroom. The room seated 1,500 people. Waitresses served dinner at long tables prior to (and sometimes during) the show.

The hotel had been considering hiring a different comedy act, one that also had a show up for network consideration. That comedy team, Rowan and Martin, had submitted their pilot for *The Rowan & Martin Show*, but it was rejected. So Carson, (who didn't yet know if he was in or out on evening network television), was hired, instead.

The Excelsior was banking on the better-known McGuire Sisters to pull in the customers. Vegas was firing on all cylinders. There was plenty of room for new talent in venues like the Excelsior, open since January of 1960. The Excelsior was still adding rooms to meet customer demand.

The new Commander's Tower was the Excelsior's latest offering. Phyllis, Dorothy and Christine were currently housed in the penthouse of this newest part of the hotel. Their separate bedrooms featured mosquito netting draped around raised platforms on which king-sized round beds rested. Christine was constantly complaining about stepping up and down to walk around the large room, which had a joint sunken conversation pit area (all the rage in interior decorating now.) There were three adjoining bedrooms with private entrances, one for each of the famous sisters.

Each sister's private bedroom/bathroom area was 700 square feet. The three bedrooms were joined by the conversation pit central seating area. White shag carpeting. A wet bar. A desk. White couches facing each other in front of a large RCA color television. The suite had a panoramic view of the Strip below. The girls could easily see their hotel neighbors, the Dunes and the Desert Inn. Across Flamingo Boulevard, the pink monstrosity of the flamingo sign for the Flamingo Hotel assaulted their fashion sense. The Flamingo had small individual cottage-like structures in back of the main casino to house its guests.

These individual Flamingo bungalows had fallen into disrepair by 1960. They made the Flamingo look dated and dilapidated when compared to the grandiose Excelsior across the boulevard, with its marble excess. Even the front entrance of the Excelsior was more impressive. It was set five hundred feet back from Flamingo Boulevard.

The Excelsior's stately cypress trees, expertly lit by night, and its white marble columns lined a 900-foot frontage entrance or winding driveway leading from Flamingo Boulevard to the Excelsior's main lobby, a majestic pathway to the main desk. Fountains and statuary abounded.

It was LaFica's intention to maintain a "classy" image, and it was The Lip's aim to be the first to spotlight up-and-coming talent. That's what motivated him to hire stars on their way up, like Carson, especially those who might soon turn up on a network television show. *The McGuire Sisters'* seven-year stay on *Arthur Godfrey's Talent Show* was part of the sisters' current crowd appeal. A shrewd businessman, The Lip hedged his bets by balancing new acts with seasoned pros like the McGuire Sisters. They were hot off the success of *Sincerely*, which charted at Number One on the Billboard Top 100.

"We don't want no has-beens at the Excelsior," the Lip had once told a news crew. "Our stars are the stars of next year. They're the future, not the past. When you come to a show at the Excelsior, you're stepping into a wholesome environment. Our guests can be proud to go home and talk about their trip. We don't got no slave girls wearing slutty costumes. We offer our guests waitresses who dress classy, like ladies. We're not gonna' be Quakers about it, but our acts and our staff are top-notch." Here, Louis gestured with his hands up, as though he were pleading with the reporters to get it right. "There's no two ways about it. We've got the McGuire sisters singing their little hearts out onstage right now. Straight out of Middletown, Ohio. America's sweethearts. You won't hear no blue language from them. Come on in. Experience Vegas entertainment the way it should be."

Ever the showman, Louis managed to get this free commercial in on his way into a Las Vegas courtroom to give a criminal deposition about a high-stakes female baccarat player who climbed on the table and danced lasciviously in the middle of a game. (The Oriental dancer eventually cost the casino $25,000 in fines levied by the Nevada Gaming Commission.) Louie was not happy about it. He banned the girl from the place forever. "It don't look good for our image. You know what I mean?" he told Sam Giancana's man in Vegas, Johnny Rosselli.

Louis "the Lip's" reputation was questionable. He was fond of saying in his own defense, "All the places out here are mobbed up. But the Excelsior is a wholesome joint. Midwesterners don't need to come here and be afraid the casino manager will pull a gun. (That happened with another casino when the inebriated star of their show insisted the stakes per hand be raised above the limit.). Customers want to know they're sitting next to somebody at a dinner show who isn't going to do somethin' stupid. They don't want nobody dangerous sittin' next to them. You know what I mean?"

"Something stupid" might be as small an offense as lighting up a cigar during a singer's act.

Dorothy looked over at Phyllis. She asked, "Did you meet Johnny Carson?"

"Yeah. He's cute, but he's taken."

"So, who did you meet that *isn't* taken?" asked Dorothy.

"Dan Rowan. Do you know him? He's a hunk."

"What's so hunk-y about him?" asked Dorothy.

"Everything." Phyllis smiled coquettishly.

Dorothy returned her youngest sister's smile and said, "Glad to hear you're going to stop hanging around with that old short Sicilian widower from Oak Park."

Phyllis' gaze darkened. "I didn't say that. You know I owe Sam. He saved my life."

Dorothy returned Phyllis' earnest gaze silently. Finally, she said, "He paid off your gambling debt, Honey. How much was it, again?"

Phyllis mumbled, "$16,000."

Once again, Dorothy snorted derisively. "Wasn't it closer to $100,000?."

"What difference does it make how much I *did* owe. I don't owe Louis 'The Lip' anything anymore. Thanks to Sam."

"Good. And you don't owe Sam Giancana anything anymore, either," responded Dorothy.

"That's not true, Dorothy. He's always been there for me. You just don't understand."

"What's to understand? He's the head of the Chicago Outfit. Has been for three years. That can't be good. You know Louie wants all of us to be squeaky clean. It's part of his image for the Excelsior. We can't afford to have it get out that you owed a big gambling debt. Or that you're going out with a known mobster."

"I'm not 'going out' with Sam. It's strictly platonic." Phyllis pouted.

"Right," Dorothy said, sarcasm coloring her voice. "And I'm in training to be a nun."

Just then, Christine entered. She was carrying shopping bags and seemed eager to share the news of her purchases. "Look at this hat," she burbled. "Doesn't it look just like the one that Jackie Kennedy was wearing in that photo in the *New York Times* last week?" Christine pulled a pillbox hat from her shopping bag. The hat featured edges that dove in and out, festooned with velvet ribbons, and complementing the light blue of the chapeau with darker blue ribbon. "It matches my blue dress with the darker blue collar. Do you think we could all three get hats alike to wear onstage?"

Dorothy again snorted derisively. "Why hats? Just because Jackie Kennedy is wearing one in a photo? Why would we be wearing hats onstage during a show? We pay hairdressers a small fortune to make our hair look good. We sit for hours getting our hair and makeup done, and then we wear hats?"

Phyllis, always the smart-ass of the group, said, "Maybe we'd be on our way to a Catholic mass. We'd have to have something on our heads." She looked from one sister to the other. Christine was still holding the blue hat in her hand. Dorothy was preparing to leave the room.

"We aren't Catholic, Phyllis. Mom was a minister at the Miamisburg First Church of God in Anderson, Indiana. How soon you forget. " Dorothy smiled, knowing that Phyllis had not been serious when she made the church comment. Lillie, their mother, really *was* a minister for a decidedly non-Catholic congregation. The sisters had begun their singing career in her church.

Phyllis was deadly serious about owing Sam Giancana. She seemed resistant to severing ties with Sam, a known member of La Cosa Nostra.

Changing the subject abruptly, Dorothy said to the newly-arrived Christine, "Guess who Phyllis has a crush on this week?"

Phyllis responded by rolling her eyes in denial. "I don't have a crush on him. I just think he's cute."

Christine, having arrived mid-conversation, said, "Who's cute?"

"Dan Rowan."

"Oooo. He is dreamy," said Christine. "And so interesting! He has the most unusual background. Generally, I don't like smokers, but he looks so distinguished when he's holding that pipe."

There wasn't a singing group in town that liked having to sing over the sound of waiters clearing dishes while smoke drifted up and choked the vocalists onstage, but smoking was all the rage. You just weren't cool if you didn't smoke.

"Wait," said Dorothy. "Why do you know this? Don't tell me you have a thing for Dan Rowan too?"

"No, I don't have a 'thing' for him, but I thought he and his partner, Dick Martin, were going to be our opening act, so I did some research. Dan Rowan was born on a carnival train in Boggs, Oklahoma. Tell me that *isn't* interesting." She looked from sister to sister. Neither contradicted her.

Both sisters were silent. Listening.

"His mom and dad died when he was only eleven. He'd been onstage with them before that. After they died, he spent four years in the McLelland Home for Boys in Pueblo, Colorado." Christine paused, but said, "And that's not even the most interesting stuff."

Phyllis bit. "What's the most interesting stuff?"

"His name isn't even Dan Rowan," said Christine.

Phyllis interrupted. "Well, what *is* his real name?"

"Daniel Hale David."

"Why did he change it?" Phyllis asked. She seemed genuinely puzzled.

"No idea," said Christine, unconcerned, putting the blue pill box hat back in her shopping bag.

Phyllis looked over at Dorothy. "Now there's an idea for you, Dorothy. Since you're so disturbed by the fact that there's another Dorothy McGuire in show business, change your name." Phyllis was smiling, although she was trying hard not to totally let her puckish sense of humor give her away. "We could be the McGuire Sisters, plus Dorothy."

"Right," said Dorothy. "I should change *my* name. Why doesn't the other Dorothy McGuire change *her* name?"

Phyllis said, "I think we already had this conversation before you arrived, Christine." Phyllis dismissed any further discussion of the two Dorothy McGuires issue by saying, "Tell us more about Dan Rowan."

"He shot down two Japanese planes and was wounded when he was shot down himself over New Guinea. He was a fighter pilot. Flew something called a Warhawk, which sounds ever so daring. Won the Distinguished Flying Cross with Oak Leaf Clusters, the Air Medal and the Purple Heart." Christine was warming to her topic.

"Wow!" said Phyllis. "All that and good-looking too."

"Well, you can forget about Dan whatever-his-last-name-is because he and his buddy aren't going to be our main act. We've got Carson, who is mucho married," groused Dorothy.

"Tonight they're not the headliners. But if they're as up-and-coming as Louie seems to think they are, maybe soon?" said Phyllis. Dorothy thought she detected a note of wistfulness in Phyllis' voice. "We should see if Louie will line up Rowan and Martin for a future gig. Maybe invite them to come see us open for Carson?"

"Is that wishful thinking on your part, Sis? Aren't you content with the many guys falling all over themselves to go out with you? Why, I read just yesterday in Sheila Graham's *Hollywood Today* column that you were sleeping with President Kennedy," said Dorothy.

Dorothy said it as though she were making a joke. She could tell instantly from the expression on Phyllis' face that she'd hit a nerve.

Rather than deny or discuss the comment, Phyllis said, "We've only got about an hour and a half before show time now. We've wasted all this time gossiping. Shouldn't we be going over the program?" Phyllis seemed irritated by her sister's offhand remark about the newly-elected President of the United States.

The trio, known for the choreographed dance moves that accompanied their singing, began briefly recapping the order of songs for that evening's show and practicing their synchronized movements to the tunes, a revolutionary approach which the Andrews Sisters and the McGuire Sisters popularized.

*

Sam "Momo" Giancana deplaned at McCarran Airport on May 30, 1960 and headed for the Excelsior, the new hotel that had opened January 1, 1960. Sam hadn't missed one of Phyllis' opening night appearances in three years.

The black-tinted limousine that picked up the colorful gangster at the airport featured a black driver holding a sign that said only "Sam."

Sam was wearing his signature fedora with the contrasting ribbon band and large dark glasses. His short, schlumpy stature could not be hidden by his expensive suit. His squatty Sicilian frame made the expensive sharkskin suit look rumpled. He sported a three-day stubble. He planned to shave before joining the McGuire Sisters for a late dinner. Sam was not a good-looking guy. You can dress a bulldog up, but it's still a bulldog.

Sam had an important meeting with a man named Robert Maheu. Maheu said he represented American interests in Cuba, corporations that had been appropriated by Castro during the 1959 revolution when many foreign businesses were nationalized by the rebels who overthrew Fulgencia Batista. Maheu contacted Johnny Rosselli, Sam Giancana's right-hand man in Vegas. The large companies wanted something done about Castro. They were losing money. Could the Mob help?

In reality, Maheu represented the CIA.

Johnny said he'd ask his boss. Sam, in turn, had his own demands. The meeting Sam was heading toward now (under the alias Sam Gold), would lay them out.

When first approached to meet Maheu, Sam said, "We should meet in Chicago. The meeting will be safer. I have Chicago under control." Maheu insisted on Las Vegas, so Sam was on his way to Louis "The Lip" LaFica's hotel, the Excelsior, where Sam "Momo" Giancana would listen to the proposed project and be present as the McGuire Sisters opened for newcomer Johnny Carson.

When Sam reached the small private conference room, the first thing he asked was, "Is this room wired?"

"No, Sir," said an agent present, Parnell McIntire. Of course, McIntire was lying. The tapes were turning and would be listened to many times over.

Parnell looked like he had just stepped off the set of a western movie, gray ten-gallon hat and all. The two men stood out in the otherwise hatless room, one wearing a fedora, one a cowboy hat. Hats were going out of style ever since JFK was pictured during the presidential campaign, hatless, his full head of hair ruffled by the breeze. The Rat Pack who affected hats now (Frank Sinatra, Peter Lawford, Dean Martin, Joey Bishop, Sammy Davis, Jr.) were still wearing fedoras like Sam's, but the hat as high fashion for men was going the way of the dodo bird.

McIntire was about as far from resembling a federal agent as you could get, which was probably why he was tapped for this job. He was a tall, handsome good old boy from McHenry County, Texas, a former Sheriff. But he was also up-and-coming in the CIA in Washington, D.C. Six foot three inches, he had a thick mane of white hair that made onlookers think of television star Lorne Greene as Ben Cartwright on *Bonanza*, which premiered in color in 1959. You could almost imagine Parnell McIntire living on the Ponderosa.

Sam was not one to waste time or mince words. He asked, "What do you want done?"

"We would like Fidel Castro to have an accident," said Parnell, with a pronounced west Texas accent.

"You want Castro whacked?" Sam said.

"We'd prefer it look as though he had an accident," Parnell repeated.

"How about poison pills?" suggested Sam. "We got some stuff that you put in food and it's lights out. Plus, we got a guy down there, Juan Orta. He's on the inside. He's inside Castro's government. He's not too happy with the way things are going. He can deliver the pills to the target." Sam paused and then added, "What's in it for me?"

"We'll pay you $150, 000," said McIntire.

"I want something else, besides," replied Sam, glancing at the dapper Johnny Rosselli seated to his left.

"What?" asked Parnell.

"I want you to bug Phyllis McGuire's dressing room. I want to know if she's seeing someone else and, if so, who." Sam lit up one of his omnipresent cigars. One of Sam's nicknames, besides "Momo," was "Sam the Cigar."

"We can do that," said Parnell, matter-of-factly. "When do you want to meet again?"

"I'll give you guys two weeks to check out what's going on backstage. The girls open for Johnny Carson tonight. You should know something in two weeks. You bring the tapes two weeks from now. I'll get the pills to Orta in Cuba after I hear what you've got. Handle your part of the bargain, and I'll make sure that Juan Orta finds his way into Fidel Castro's kitchen," said Giancana, rising from the table and extending his hand to shake Parnell McIntire's.

"You've got a deal," said Parnell, reaching down from his much greater height to shake the older man's hand.

*

Backstage before Opening Night is nerve-wracking. It was nervous-time right after the hotel opened, and it would be butterflies

73

again tonight, as the McGuire Sisters opened for Johnny Carson.

Carson came out and did a noticeably blue joke. "I had a girlfriend in high school who had an angora sweater. We were parked on Lovers' Lane once. We were there for quite a while," said Carson, as he adjusted his cuffs, a tic he often incorporated into his act. "When her head came back up, it looked like a chicken had exploded in my lap."

Louis The Lip laughed nervously from the back of the packed room; he was assessing how this racy material was going over with the crowd, after he had bragged about the wholesome shows at the Excelsior.

Seguing smoothly, Carson went on more innocently, "You know the sound a sheep makes when it explodes?" He looked expectantly around the room; no one responded. "Sis Boom B-a-a-a-h." He punctuated the sheep sound punchline with the boy-next-door smile that millions would come to know and love during Carson's years on the *Tonight Show with Johnny Carson*, 4,531 episodes that commenced in 1962. Johnny was still "the Great Carson-I" from Iowa and Nebraska in spirit, the little boy who wanted to be a magician when he grew up.

The McGuire Sisters were pros. They were prepared, as always. Phyllis, however, was particularly jittery, because she knew that Sam "Momo" Giancana was there. She liked Sam very much. She also liked Dan Rowan very much, but not in the same way. Phyllis was concerned. The paths of the two men must not cross. She would do everything she could to keep Sam in the dark about any other suitors. She knew intuitively that Sam was territorial and possessive.

Rowan was everything that Giancana was not. He was handsome, six foot two inches with dark wavy hair. Smart. Charming. A war hero. Sam was just stubby little Sam. Phyllis knew that a puppy could turn on its master and rip its throat out if the pup were mistreated. Sam's puppy-dog-like devotion to her could go south if she misbehaved. She would have to be on her best behavior.

Lately, Phyllis had been misbehaving, most of the time with Dan Rowan. She had personally invited the handsome half of the comedy duo to come see the sisters open for Carson. "Why bother going through our manager?" she said to Dorothy and Christine. "I'll just pop over to the Sands. Rowan and Martin hang out there. I'll see if I can deliver the message personally. They'll be more likely to come if I ask them myself. Maybe I can float the idea of teaming up for a future show."

Phyllis had been successful in more ways than one. Perhaps a bit too successful for her own future good.

Just then, the very handsome man she was thinking about, knocked on her dressing room door.

"Are you decent?" a pleasant male voice asked.

"As decent as I'm likely to get," answered Phyllis with a small laugh, letting the questioner make up his own mind.

The door opened slightly, and Phyllis rose to greet the handsome straight man of the Rowan & Martin comedy team. Like Martin and Lewis, Dan was the Dean Martin good looking one, while Dick Martin was Jerry Lewis, the less-good-looking funny man.

As far as Phyllis was concerned, Dan Rowan put Dean Martin's looks to shame. Phyllis wasn't a fan of boozy married Italians and had steered clear, so far, of both Martin and Sinatra. She might make an exception for a married Irish politician who also just happened to be President of the United States. John Fitzgerald Kennedy was married, yes, but he and his lovely wife, Jacqueline, seemed to have an arrangement that allowed JFK more leeway than most married men. Phyllis couldn't deny that she found the Harvard-educated Boston boy from the big Irish Catholic family charming, but she was not nearly as turned on by his attention as she was by the thought of Dan Rowan, the handsome single man now approaching her. His touch left her weak in the knees, and Phyllis wasn't usually a weak-in-the-knees kind of girl.

Phyllis could feel herself growing warm all over in anticipation of Dan Rowan's embrace. She knew that this was not a convenient time to have those old familiar feelings.

Dan moved gracefully to Phyllis' side. He slid both arms around her waist. "You nervous, honey?" he asked the beautiful brunette.

She could smell the faint aroma of the expensive pipe tobacco blend Rowan smoked. The odor was so much better than Sam Giancana's smelly Cuban cigars. Phyllis knew she couldn't stay in Dan Rowan's arms too long. If she did, she'd want to stay there forever.

"I'm nervous when you're holding me like this. I just spent two hours in hair and makeup." Phyllis said, pulling away. Her excuse was not the complete truth.

Rowan laughed, a hearty male sound that boomed in the small

room. "Hey, don't be nervous because *I'm* here. Be nervous because soon you'll be out *there*," said Rowan, gesturing toward the door that led to the stage. Then the conversation turned serious. "I wanted to ask you something, Phyllis. I'm having a birthday on July 22nd. I'd like you to go with me to France. I'm taking a look at a barge that is permanently moored in the Seine in Paris. It might be a great retirement idea to spend part of the year on this barge. Part of it in some warm state. California. Florida. Maybe even here in Vegas."

"Oh, Dan. I don't know if I can get away from the Excelsior for that long. We're set up as the opening act for almost any new talent that Louie thinks is going to be big in the near future. I'm going to have to check. See what the girls have to say." She busied herself replacing the few strands of hair that had fallen out of place when she kissed the handsome interloper and snuggled on his comfortable chest. Her heart was beating faster than before Rowan's entrance, and Phyllis felt herself falling under his spell. She wanted to say, "Yes! I'd *love* to go with you to Paris." That would be her heart talking.

What Phyllis was really thinking, what her head was saying was, *I'm going to have to see if I can get away with this. If Sam finds out, there'll be hell to pay.*

"I don't need an answer right this minute, Phyllis. But I'd sure like to take my girl to see Paris. You ever been to Paris, Phyllis?" Rowan tilted his head and gave her an appraising look as he asked this question. He seemed both inquisitive and admiring. He touched her chin and tilted her lovely face up toward his, moving in for a kiss before Phyllis could disentangle herself.

"No, I haven't, but I've always wanted to go. And I'd rather go with you than with anyone in the world." Phyllis had no difficulty saying this with complete sincerity. Sam had mentioned taking her to France, but she had demurred. Sam told her, "Someday, Phyllis, I'll build you your very own Eiffel Tower here in the U.S." (Sam made good on that promise.) Dan's proposal was different, in Phyllis' heart and mind.

Phyllis was not some innocent or naïve ingénue. She had been around. She knew the score. She was worried about Sam Giancana's line of work. He might have made his reputation as a wheelman, but plenty of tough guys worked for him who did not confine their talents to simply driving the get-away car.

Phyllis didn't want to endanger Dan Rowan. She also had less-romantic affection for the schlumpy little guy whose dad once operated a food pushcart in west Chicago. Sam had been more than kind to her. She didn't want to hurt him and she didn't want *him* to hurt *her.*

More importantly, she didn't want Sam to come down hard on Dan Rowan simply for inviting her to accompany him to France. Sam must not find out about the invitation, even if Phyllis declined it. *Who knows what Sam would do?*

*

When Dorothy left the white-carpeted central lounge area for the privacy of her own bedroom, her mind was filled with a variety of concerns. There was tonight's show. There was Dan Rowan. There was Sam Giancana. *And why did Phyllis react the way she did when I mentioned a romance with JFK?* Dorothy knew nothing about such a liaison. She wasn't sure she wanted to confirm it, if it was true. It sounded like more trouble for the McGuire Sisters.

Dorothy needed time to unwind, and a little less time playing the cautious older sister. It was a role she knew well, having served in that capacity for three decades, but even a warden or a headmistress deserves a few days off. Christine didn't have the temperament to ride herd on her two sisters, so Dorothy, the middle sister, inherited the Mother Hen role.

Dorothy decided that she'd spend some time in the casino after the show, in those areas of the casino that were reserved only for high rollers and important people, where celebrities would be shielded from the stares of the common folk.

She picked up the phone in her bedroom to check with Louis "The Lip" LaFica. Louie would tell her where the hotel's most important guests were going to be hanging out after the show. And that's where she met the enchanting Lorne Greene look-alike in the gray ten-gallon cowboy hat, Parnell McIntire.

*

Several drinks and many hours after the successful opening night for the McGuire Sisters and Johnny Carson, Dorothy found herself

completely enthralled with Parnell McIntire. He was charming. Old
School. A gentleman. Even though she had a boyfriend back in Ohio,
she couldn't help but be entranced with this tall, handsome stranger.
At thirty-four, she was old enough to enjoy his company for as long
as he was willing to escort her about town.

"How long are you going to be in Las Vegas?" she asked Parnell
as they parted that first night.

"I'll be here at least two weeks. Maybe more," Parnell said,
undressing the singer with his eyes. His liquid brown eyes displayed
great intelligence, mixed with so many other desirable traits that
Dorothy found herself falling under Parnell's spell.

She joked, "There's something about a man in a ten-gallon
hat…" Parnell just laughed, a manly sound. Dorothy said, "You
remind me of Lorne Greene, the actor, only you have a better head
of hair."

Parnell laughed again. "I'll take that as a compliment, then."

"You should, because it is," Dorothy countered. She really liked
this guy. She asked, "What, exactly, brings you to Vegas, anyway?"

Parnell gave a vague answer. "Business," he said.

At first, Parnell lied to her about his true line of work. But, as
time passed, the wine flowed, and they were together on many other
dates, he began to trust the most sensible McGuire sister and wanted
to share more with her. He trusted her to be silent. He also had
concerns for Dorothy's sister, Phyllis.

Parnell couldn't, in good conscience, continue to let Dorothy's
youngest sister consort with a dangerous mobster without
emphasizing to someone in a position to dissuade her from her
foolish actions that hanging out with Sam Giancana was potentially
disastrous. Dorothy was that voice of reason that might cry in the
Vegas wilderness. She had the best chance of persuading Phyllis to
stop seeing Sam Giancana.

Dorothy had already mentioned her displeasure over her sister's
romance with the older widower in casual conversation. Repeatedly.
Parnell knew that they were on the same page when it came to the
ultimate end goal. If Dorothy had the sort of influence with Phyllis
that she now had with him, maybe he could do a good deed.

He decided to fill Dorothy in on the real reason he was in Las
Vegas and his real line of work, even though it was dangerous for
him to do so.

It was late on the night of their fourth or fifth date, all of them after-show dates that often ended up becoming all-nighters, that Parnell chose to tell Dorothy about the Fidel Castro assassination attempt offer made to Sam Giancana. He didn't make the decision to share this sensitive information lightly. He knew he might be blowing up his own career in the process.

"Sam said he'd kill Castro. Probably using poison pills. But he had another condition," Parnell said.

"What condition?" Dorothy asked.

Parnell gave Dorothy an intent look. "Sam said he wanted your sister Phyllis' dressing room bugged. It has, in fact, been bugged for the past week."

Dorothy was dumbstruck upon learning that her sister's words and actions in her private dressing room were being monitored. She had no illusions about Sam's harmlessness (delusions which Phyllis seemed to entertain). When Sam found out everything that went on in Phyllis' dressing room, no one was safe.

"Oh, no!" she exclaimed when Parnell broke the news to her. "Dan Rowan is in there with Phyllis almost every night. There's no telling what he and Phyllis are talking about. Or doing. If Sam hears those tapes, Rowan is a dead man." The terrified look on Dorothy's face spoke volumes.

Parnell continued, "This is Top Secret in the agency, Dorothy. I could lose my job if they knew I'd shared this information with you or with anybody else. Right now, it's strictly speculative. Sam has agreed to kill Castro using poison. There have actually been eight different plots against Castro that have been proposed. One, Operation Mongoose, went right to the top. Bobby Kennedy was going to cooperate. He'd allow justice to collaborate with the Mob to kill Castro. But Sam Giancana hasn't bought into an even worse plot suggested to him yet. Something we know about from wiretaps in Chicago.

There's a move by organized crime to rid itself of the Kennedys. You know that Bobby has been sending more mobsters to jail than any Attorney General in history. Old Joe made a deal with the Mafia. He said he'd call off his son's if the Mob helped Kennedy win West Virginia, which the Outfit did. If, for any reason, JFK and RFK don't honor their father's pledge, there's going to be a concerted Mob effort to get rid of the Kennedys.

The CIA has Sam on tape telling one of JFK's girlfriends, Judith Exner, 'Your boyfriend wouldn't be in the White House if it weren't for me.' Sam expressed how upset he was at the way Bobby Kennedy was going after the Mob. Sam said, "We broke our balls for him and gave him the election, and he gets his brother to hound us to death.' Sam sounded really, really angry."

Parnell directed a searching look at Dorothy, to see how she was handling all this sensitive information.

Dorothy's mouth opened wide in horror. "You don't mean killing Jack or Bobby, do you?"

"I didn't say that, Dorothy, but the Mob got rid of Anton Cermak, the Mayor of Chicago, back in the thirties. They're certainly more powerful right now. But they won't continue to be if Bobby Kennedy keeps the pressure on. All I know is that your sister is mixed up with a guy who is capable of anything. If you have any influence with her, get her to stay away from Giancana, especially now."

With those parting words, Parnell McIntire left Dorothy at the door to her suite within the Excelsior.

Dorothy was up almost all night, thinking about the implications of what Parnell had confided. She could think of only one way to save Dan Rowan's life and, perhaps, her little sister's as well. She must set up a private meeting with Sam. Tell him what she knew about his intentions confidentially. Threaten to expose him to the authorities if he moved against Dan or anyone else.

She knew she'd be putting her own life in danger, but, if she didn't do something, once Sam Giancana heard the tapes made in Phyllis' dressing room, Dan Rowan would be like a clay pigeon in a shooting gallery. Who knew? Even Phyllis might not be safe. And more important figures might be next. Phyllis had fallen for Dan Rowan hard. She had asked Dorothy if she could accompany Rowan to Paris on his July birthday trip.

Maybe I can kill two birds with one stone, thought Dorothy. If I reveal what I know about Sam's intentions to Sam, yes, it will put me at risk, but Sam loves Phyllis and Phyllis wouldn't take kindly to Sam murdering me. I have to do it, for Phyllis' sake, for Dan Rowan's sake, for the sake of even more prominent targets.

Dorothy made a vow to set up a private meeting with Sam as soon as possible. Since all three of the sisters were to dine with Sam tomorrow night before their latest show at 9 p.m., she would get Sam alone and ask him then.

Maybe set up a meeting with Sam just before Phyllis and Christine arrive, Dorothy thought.

*

The first week's run of the new Carson show had set box office records for the Excelsior. Johnny had done well, with the help of Phyllis, Dorothy and Christine McGuire. He tied with Liberace's attendance, a benchmark. Liberace made $50,000 a week appearing at the Riviera at the opposite end of the Strip.

It was to celebrate the success of new-comer Carson's opening that all three of the McGuire Sisters met with Sam Giancana for dinner in the elegant dining room of the Excelsior, the Empire Room.

Dorothy contacted Sam privately by phone prior to their 7:30 p.m. dinner reservations.

"Sam, could you meet me for a drink in the Empire Room about 6:30?"

"Sure, Dorothy. What's up?" Sam asked affably.

"I just wanted to have a chance to talk with you privately before Phyllis and Christine join us. You know how chatty those two are." Dorothy chuckled, as though she had nothing serious to discuss.

"No problem, Dorothy. Anything you girls want or need, you just let me know."

Sam had no idea that Dorothy knew what he was up to regarding bugging Phyllis' dressing room or anything else.

One hour before the trio's dinner reservations, Dorothy entered the Empire Room alone. She saw Sam seated in a corner booth capable of seating at least eight people. Large, overstuffed booths were used down front for important guests at many of the Strip's venues, and, as often as not, the booths were filled with one or two Mob figures invested in the Sands or the Sahara or the Dunes or the Flamingo or any of a number of smaller casinos on the Strip, downtown, or in neighboring Henderson.

Dorothy was dressed in a slinky black cocktail dress with a short skirt and three-inch high stiletto heels. She carried a black clutch purse, wore dangly diamond earrings and a diamond necklace, and carried a light black glittery shawl to compensate for the air conditioning. It was May. Had it been January, when the Excelsior first opened, Dorothy would have been draped in her mink stole, but the temperatures outside were soaring and she only needed the shawl to offset the air conditioning draft.

"What's up, Dorothy? What's on your mind?" Sam asked. Never one to beat around the bush or waste words, he was curious.

Dorothy, too, believed in being direct. "Sam, I know you're bugging Phyllis' dressing room." She waited to see if Sam denied the charge. He did not. "No matter what you hear or think you hear, no matter how happy or angry her words make you, you have to let Phyllis live her life the way she wants to live her life. If she leaves you, she was never yours to begin with. If you set her free to make her own choices and she genuinely loves you, she'll come back to you." Dorothy knew she was not the original author of those sentiments, but they were the right ones for the situation.

Sam looked weary and old beyond his years. He was fifty-two years old to Phyllis' twenty-nine. It wasn't uncommon for rich older men to squire younger starlet arm candy in Vegas, but a twenty-three year age gap was a big gap. Dan Rowan was thirty-eight, nine years older than Phyllis. It was true that Sam was old enough to be Phyllis' father. Sam's daughter, Antoinette, was twenty-five, four years younger than Phyllis.

Sam didn't flinch. He listened thoughtfully and removed a cigar from his inner jacket pocket. "Does Phyllis know you're here talking to me about this?" Sam asked Dorothy. He had a world-weary look in his eyes, but he did not appear angry.

"Not only does she not know I'm talking to you about the recordings, she doesn't even know she's being bugged. And I haven't told her. Whatever you hear on those tapes when they're delivered to you (Dorothy knew from Parnell that Sam had not yet heard them) is the private life of a twenty-nine-year-old single woman who has every right to live her life the way she sees fit. Phyllis cares about you, Sam. I know she does. But she's young. She wants to take a trip to France with a friend who has invited her. She wants to sow some wild oats. She wants to do all sorts of things that we all want to do when we're young. She should have that opportunity." As she rushed through this impromptu speech, Dorothy was as nervous as she had been ten minutes before show time on opening night.

"Why haven't you told her about the bugging?" asked Sam.

"Why should I? She can say and do anything she wants, within reason. She's not doing anything illegal." Dorothy regretted that last remark as soon as it left her lips, but it was too late to recall it.

"You're implying that I am doing something illegal?" Sam said, calmly, as he cut the tip off the cigar he was preparing to light up.

"Let's not go there, Sam. I don't know anything about your business dealings, and that's the way I want to keep it. But I do know about one important deal that you've been asked to potentially set up in Texas. So help me, if you meddle in Phyllis' private life, if you tell her she isn't allowed to travel wherever she wants to go, with whomever she wants, whenever she wants, I'll tell the intended target of that Texas attack. I'll tell him personally, to his face. I just hope to God that what I heard about Texas was just hearsay."

"Where *did* you get this information, Dorothy? It seems as though there's a rat in the woodwork somewhere." Sam did not appear angry, but the wheels were definitely turning in his head. "Of course it's all hearsay. Who did you hear it from?"

"You know I'll never tell you that, Sam. Let's just say that a little bird told me. And now, if you'll excuse me, I have to go upstairs to rendezvous with the girls for our 7:30 dinner date with a very nice man from Chicago." Dorothy rose, preparing to leave. Her legs were actually wobbly as she prepared to totter toward the elevators.

Sam smiled, lit up his cigar, and said, "You always were the smart one, Dorothy. You're just like a mother to your sisters. Phyllis has told me that more than once. Don't worry. I'll keep cool no matter what I hear on those tapes. And I don't know from nothing about Texas. There is no Texas on my to-do list. Capisce?" Sam smiled through clouds of cigar smoke at Dorothy, who was now trembling at the very idea that she had faced down one of the world's most dangerous men and come away unscathed.

She was too frightened to look back at the small man in the big booth as she approached the elevators to her penthouse suite on rubbery legs.

*

Carson's run at the Excelsior was over. A radiant Phyllis McGuire was heading for McCarran International Airport with Dan

Rowan, en route to Paris, France. It was July 10, 1960. The McGuire Sisters had a hiatus from the Excelsior until August.

Phyllis snuggled up next to the handsome Rowan in the cab. She said, "I'm really looking forward to this trip, Dan. You don't know how long I've wanted to visit Paris. I'm surprised that Dorothy said I could go for two weeks, but I'm not going to second-guess the boss." She smiled in happy contentment.

"Everyone should visit Paris at least once, Phyllis. I'm just glad that you'll be seeing it for the first time with me, honeybunch. It will be as though I'm seeing everything for the first time all over again. I love Paris. I do plan to retire at least part of the time there, God willing and the river don't rise."

Phyllis laughed. "Where did you get that expression, Dan?"

"Who knows, honey? You bring out my poetic side. Or my Oklahoma side. Definitely my romantic side. I can hardly wait to get you alone on the Eiffel Tower. It's a fantastic view of the city of love. We'll celebrate my thirty-eighth birthday in style. It might be a very long night. Are you ready for that?" He smiled at her and added, "And I hope we celebrate many more birthdays together."

His left hand touched her back. They were now seated next to one another on the TWA airliner in close proximity in first class, awaiting champagne. His hand moved upward. Under her lightweight top. Over bare skin. Skimming the back of her bra. They sat together, temporarily alone, waiting for Dom Perignon to be served them by a TWA uniformed flight attendant. Phyllis felt the heat rising in her body. It wasn't from the champagne bubbling in elegant flute glasses.

"I'm ready, willing and able," replied the smitten singer. She touched the top of Dan's left thigh as he sat comfortably in the airplane seat next to her. It was hard for either of them to keep their hands off each other. The mutual impulse was to passionately embrace, but they were in public.

Momentarily alone, the two indulged in a quick passionate kiss that left no doubt about how Dorothy McGuire and Dan Rowan would spend Rowan's thirty-eighth birthday in Paris.

6

THERE WILL ALWAYS BE VEGAS

Mathew Kaufman

Arthur Westbrooke

"Welcome to the Excelsior, Mr. Westbrooke. How was your flight in?" Jackson inquired, stepping out of the limo.

"Fine. Fine. How's the casino host business?" Westbrooke asked.

Polite conversation... At times, it feels like the whole god-damned world is fake. Being a wealthy businessman had taught Arthur Westbrooke how to converse with almost anyone in, well, almost any situation. It was how he first met Jackson.

Late one evening in 1999, Arthur had gotten far too intoxicated and began gambling obnoxious amounts of money at the blackjack tables. Twenty-five-dollar hands quickly progressed to one-hundred-, two-hundred-, three-hundred-dollar hands. Jackson was assigned as his host after the money began raining in.

Arthur was merely a lonely, traveling pharmaceutical salesman at the time. Albeit, one of the best in the world. But being good at your job surely does not mean you are good at your life. The attention Jackson had given him made Arthur feel welcome and less lonely. That was a nice change.

Arthur's income was well into the high six figures by that time in his life, and after years of unbridled saving and good investments, he was a millionaire. None of that mattered to him though. He just wanted to not be lonely, so he returned to Las Vegas and the Excelsior Resort roughly once or twice a quarter, depending on business.

Dating was meaningless and almost a bothersome, hopeless formality. It seemed that every relationship derailed at nearly the same point—the beginning. He wanted to date, but men were busy. Society in the eighties demanded that men be men. There was no room for a high-level corporate queer. So he quit trying to date and poured all of himself into his work. Arthur had been promoted almost yearly until he reached Chairman and CEO of Diamond Pharmaceuticals. His heart grew colder as his wallet grew thicker.

Men would gladly sleep with Arthur, and the comfort of a male prostitute filled the hole in his heart for short periods of time. There were even a few working men who he stayed in contact with when he left town. Until they stopped answering his calls.

In the early nineties, an asshole escort reminded him that they were not, in fact, friends or lovers. The arrogant tight-bodied thirty-something little shit had the audacity to tell Arthur, "Listen, gramps, I don't date saggy old men." Saggy old men… That was that. The quest for love was over. Arthur knew he would die alone, as a saggy old man, rather than endure the heart-wrenching feelings of insults like that ever again.

After all, there would always be Vegas.

Hunter Grady

Hunter grabbed a bell cart and wheeled it to the back of the long black limousine. The driver fumbled in his pocket as he moved toward the back and removed the keys from his pocket. With an audible click, the trunk sprang open.

"Mr. Westbrooke is in suite 50-113. He is a good tipper so I would hurry straight to his room if you want something like this," the driver said, flashing two crisp one-hundred-dollar bills to Hunter.

"Jesus. That's awesome!" Hunter said.

The driver nodded as Hunter loaded the bags onto the cart: two large suitcases and a thick garment bag, Armani displayed vividly across the front of it. *He really does have money!*

Once secure, Hunter pushed the bell cart across the drive and into the Excelsior. The cart slid gracefully across the polished marble flooring. Hunter pushed it past the front desk and through the casino. Brilliant LED and neon lights lit up the slots as he passed.

It was only seven-thirty p.m. and the casino guests were already filling the casino floor. Sounds of bells and excited laughter filled the air. The smell of booze and cheap cigars drifted past him. Hunter dodged the groups of patrons until he arrived at the door leading to the service elevators in the back of house. He pushed the button for the fiftieth floor. The doors closed and the elevator car began to ascend swiftly.

Hunter had always loved riding in elevators. Each time he did, his face lit up. He could still remember his first elevator ride as a kid. It was in Maxfield Mall, and it he thought it was so much fun that he begged his mom and dad to take him on it three more times that day.

Hunter smiled as the car slowed, eventually stopping on fifty. He lugged the cart out and pushed it from the service lobby into the hall. A minute or so later, he found himself standing in front of 50-113. He adjusted his black uniform jacket and knocked.

Footsteps approached from inside the room. The door cracked open. A sideways head and two eyes appeared.

"Mr. Westbrooke?"

"Yes."

"I have your luggage, sir. Where would you like it?"

"Oh, very good. Please, bring it in and put it in the closet." He opened the door and waved him in. "That was fast. I wasn't expecting you for another half-hour," Mr. Westbrooke said.

"I have lots of luggage to deliver, sir. It's best not to dawdle."

"Ah, an industrious boy, much like myself when I was your age," he said.

Hunter turned just in time to see his smile. It was the most amazing, perfect smile. He shook it off, grabbed the luggage and moved it to the closet. He turned to tell Mr. Westbrooke he was all set, but he was gone. *I have to be losing my mind.*

"Mr. Westbrooke?" Hunter said.

He stepped out of the bathroom wearing a T-shirt and wrapped in a towel.

"Sir, your luggage is put away. Have a great day." He grabbed the cart and pushed it toward the door.

Mr. Westbrooke cut him off, "Grab my wallet and take three hundred out. You were very fast and I appreciate that."

"Oh, sir, I don't feel comfortable—"

"Just do it. It's not like you are going to steal from me. The wallet is on the dresser. Show yourself out when you are done. Thanks again!" he hollered.

He heard the glass shower door close, presumably after Westbrooke stepped in. Did he really just leave him, a stranger, alone with his wallet in his room and tell him to take three hundred-dollars? Hunter went toward the wallet but thought better of it. Sure, he wanted the money, but he wanted to keep his job too.

For some reason, he thought of that smile and grinned as he walked out of the suite. What was that?

Arthur Westbrooke

Fantastic shower. It was almost eight-thirty when Arthur finished. Stepping out of the shower, he wrapped himself with the plush, white, cotton towel. The room had a welcoming feel to him. More than most other hotels he had stayed in.

Arthur pulled his luggage to the dresser and opened the drawer. Sliding the clothes in the drawer, he noticed his wallet looked untouched. *Did he even take a tip?* Pausing from putting his clothes away, Arthur inventoried the wallet. *Nothing is missing. He didn't take a dime. Interesting…*

Smiling, he retrieved the phone and began dialing.

"Good evening, Mr. Westbrooke. How may I help you today?" a voice spoke.

"I have a bit of an odd request. There was a bellman that brought up my luggage. I forgot to give him a tip. Could you send him back up? I also need a bottle of Maker's Mark; would you send

88

that up with him also?"

"Absolutely sir. Is there anything else that I may assist you with?"

"No, ma'am. I believe that will be all. Thank you."

"You are very welcome, sir. I will get the items right up to you. Thank you for choosing the Excelsior."

The line cleared with a quiet click and he returned the phone to the cradle. *I admire the honesty. It is such a rare trait these days.*

Westbrooke filled the ice bucket from the machine down the hallway. He laid out two rocks glasses and retired to the couch, clicking on the television as he sat. He selected a jazz classics station and let his mind drift.

Hunter Grady

Traffic in the front drive whizzed by Hunter. He happily pulled a new arrival's luggage across the lanes. *Why am I so happy?* He had practically been whistling Dixie since he left Mr. Westbrooke's suite.

Sure, the guy was cute, but he was way older than Hunter. And sure, he offered him a three-hundred-dollar tip but, he didn't even take it. Seriously, there wasn't really anything to be that happy about?

Hunter had just turned nineteen and had only been working as a bellboy for six months or so. It was the first job he had that paid him above the table. The first job he had that didn't run the risk of a criminal conviction.

It's not that he was a criminal by nature. But there comes a point in life where you would do one of two things: fight to live or lay down and die. Hunter was strong and would do anything for his family so, obviously, he fought.

His dad had passed away when he was just five and his mom… His poor mom had been left to care for him and his younger brother, Rory, who was just an infant when his father passed. They had been on and off food stamps and housing assistance almost as long as he could remember.

It wasn't until his mom had a stroke on Hunter's sixteenth birthday and she lost the ability to walk and talk that things really fell apart. Luckily, she regained the ability to talk but, sadly, that was it. He loved his mother, so he had vowed to do whatever needed to be done.

At first, he tried to get odd jobs around the neighborhood, delivering groceries and running errands. But a sixteen-year-old can only find so much to do in Las Vegas, and really, how much money could he make? Certainly not enough to be the sole income for a family of three.

It didn't take long until he found himself being pulled into a bad crowd. One evening, while walking home from an evening of deliveries, he cut through an alley just off Twain Avenue. It was dark out already and the narrow alley made things even darker. Usually it wasn't a big deal and he was able to swiftly pass through. That night was different.

Hunter found himself surrounded by a group of muscle-bound black men. They began badgering him, at first asking simple questions like why he was out late all alone. That soon progressed to more leading questions about being gay and blowing dudes.

The men drug Hunter behind an enclosed dumpster and had their way with him. From that night on, for a little over a year, Hunter was forced into male-male prostitution. He reported nightly to his pimp Ty-Ty and was given a burner cell that Ty-Ty would call him on when he had a trick.

It was fucking awful... Sort of. Yeah, it sucked dick that he had to suck dick. But he did get to suck dick. Sometimes the trick was a well-off middle-aged married guy with kids and a family. He preferred them. They were usually nice. Sometimes it was a bunch of strung out druggies looking for an ass to run a train on. Those nights were the worst.

It wasn't all bad though. Ty-Ty paid him enough to take care of his mom and little brother. It was nowhere near what the tricks were paying, but at least he could provide for his family. Until Ty-Ty went to jail anyway. That gave him the out he needed. The damage to his self-esteem was already done, though. He was depressed and now jobless.

Immediately, he started looking for work and was lucky enough to charm his way into the Excelsior. Life was better, but inside, he was still a wreck. But anyways...

Hunter's radio chirped, "Hunter, Suite 50-113 needs a bottle of Maker's. I know you are not supposed to, but he requested you deliver it," the dispatcher said.

"Copy that," he replied. Hunter grabbed the bottle and hopped into the staged elevator. *Why does he want me? I didn't take any money. What could he want?*

Arthur Westbrooke

Arthur sipped his drink. The cool liquid went down with a bite as he gazed out the window and watched the glowing neon lights of Las Vegas. Crowds of ant-like people marched up and down both sides of the Strip. Arthur was glad he was up here and they way down there, although a part of him longed for a human connection.

His crowd gazing was interrupted by a knock at the door. A muffled voice pierced the door.

"Guest Services," the voice said.

Arthur recognized the voice immediately. *Hunter.* Arthur's palms instantaneously drenched with nervous sweat. *Jesus, pull yourself together, man. It's just a boy. Albeit, a rather cute boy, but come on...*

Arthur wiped his hands dry on his khakis as he walked to the door. He grabbed the door handle. It was shockingly cool to the touch. He paused before opening the one barrier that separated him from Hunter. *Here we go.* The door opened with a slight creak.

Oh my God... His breath left his body as Hunter appeared. Hunter's face lit up with his perfect, cute little smile. It was mesmerizing, and Arthur had to try his hardest not to stare creepily at him. Although he wasn't sure just how successful he was with that, as Hunter had to speak first.

"Good Evening, Mr. Westbrooke. Here is the Maker's Mark you requested."

"Oh, right. Thank you," Arthur replied. "Please come in. Let me get you a drink. Can you stay for a drink?"

"Oh, um... Sure. I just got off work now. This was my last delivery."

"Wonderful, please then, come in. What is your drink of choice?"

"I'll have... whatever you are having."

Arthur took note of the young man's nervousness but was not sure what caused it. He was just as bad at reading social situations as he was at being in them. *Oh well.* Hunter was here now and he had to try his hardest to make the most of just being in his company.

"Please, sit." Arthur gestured to the seating area near the window.

Hunter selected the leather armchair that sat directly across from the sofa and sunk into it, obviously startled.

Arthur snickered. "Yeah. Don't feel bad. I did the same damn thing. The chair almost swallowed me. I'd offer the couch to you, but it will probably take you twenty minutes to escape the chair."

Hunter smiled again, causing Arthur to feel tingly inside. Almost like a nervous child. The feeling started in his belly and spread out as far as his fingertips. He felt himself blush. He quickly turned away and poured Hunter a glass of Maker's and topped off his own as well.

"So, how was work?" Arthur awkwardly inquired.

"Oh, it was good. I met a lot of new people today and rode the elevator like a hundred times!" Hunter blurted out.

"You like riding the elevators?"

"Oh yeah, it is the best part of my job. I mean, I love meeting the people, but people... Well, people are really awful sometimes and they really let ya down. An elevator though... Well let's just say, I haven't ever been let down by an elevator, unless I asked it to."

The simple realness of Hunter shocked Arthur. *I could never have imagined a young man with the sweetness that he has.* He joined Hunter in the sitting area and passed him the drink before he sat on the sofa.

"Thanks," Hunter said.

"You are very welcome. So, do you know why I asked you to come tonight?"

"Well, I assumed it is because you needed some Maker's Mark. Is that right?"

"Incidentally, yes, I suppose there is that, but I also wanted to inquire as to why you didn't take any money from my wallet when I offered you a tip. Surely your wages cannot be so great as to pass on the opportunity to make a few-hundred-dollar tip."

Hunter's face flushed, "No, sir. That isn't the case at all. You see, I could use the money but, well... " Hunter paused and turned even more red.

"What is it? Are you ok?"

Hunter Grady

Hunter raised his hand to his partially cover his face. "No. I mean, yes, I'm fine."

Hunter had a sickening feeling in the pit of his stomach. He felt an attraction to this man, felt safe conversing with him. He even felt like he *could* tell him anything but, why?

Rather than divulging any information to Arthur, Hunter changed the subject. "So, do you visit Vegas often?"

"Oh… Yes. Yes I do. I am here several times a year. But I am not always as lucky as I was today," Arthur replied.

"Lucky? Lucky how?"

"I have never had the pleasure of meeting such a beautiful young man like yourself."

Hunter felt his face heat to the temperature of the sun. He imagined that he must look like a very embarrassed tomato.

"I, uh. Well, wow. Thank you," Hunter stuttered. "I thought you were very handsome when I came in as well." Hunter smiled uncontrollably.

"And that, that smile right there, is why I had to see you again. I saw that very same grin as I tightened the towel around my waist earlier. I was hoping that meant you were like me." Arthur leaned in for a quick kiss.

Hunter pushed away, tears filling his eyes." I'm very sorry, sir, I'm not like you. I have to go."

Hunter stood and took one last look at Arthur. He, of course was a little like him. He was gay, and he was attracted to Arthur. But that was where the similarities stopped. Arthur was rich, successful, and good looking. All he was, was a broken, poor boy, with baggage. Lots of baggage.

Hunter set the glass on the table. It was so quiet in the room that the click of the glass on the table sounded like a plane crash. Tears flowed freely down Hunter's cheeks as he ran out the door.

Arthur Westbrooke

"Wait! Don't go!" he yelled. But it was already too late. The door slammed closed behind Hunter.

FUCK! Son of a bitch! Arthur ran to the door and jerked it open,

93

but it was already too late. Hunter's footsteps slapped across the marble floor near the elevators already. *This is why I don't try to meet people. I always screw things up.*

Arthur flipped off the lights and returned to the couch. Drink in hand and soft jazz still playing, he began to quietly weep.

*

Morning came with a headache, a broken drinking glass, and a stiff neck. Arthur awoke on the couch. The same place he had sat last night. Shit. Hunter. It took Arthur a while to clear the fog of last night's drinking. The shower helped though. Sort of.

All it did was remind him of Hunter. Everything in his suite reminded him of Hunter. I have to get out of this room. *I have to clear my head.* With that, he dressed and readied himself for the day. He didn't have any plans so he headed to the elevators.

A short ride later Arthur found himself standing on the Excelsior's polished marble floors. Slot machines honked and rang, and people filled them with their hard-earned money. *I'll try the concierge. Maybe they will have an idea to take my mind off him.*

Several minutes later, he arrived at the concierge desk. "Ah, good afternoon, sir," a gentleman in a black wool suit said from behind the desk. "How may I assist you?"

"Are there any shows going on tonight? I have to get out for a bit," Arthur inquired.

"Yes, of course, sir. Is there anything in particular you would like to see?"

"No. I was hoping you could give me some suggestions."

"Absolutely. You are in luck actually. The famous journalist Hunter S. Thompson is having a show here tonight. I have a flyer."

The man reached in the desk, retrieved it, and passed it across the desk. *Fear and Loathing in America: The Journals of Hunter S. Thompson.*

Arthur could feel his eyes dilate as his brain began to whir. Hunter. Damn. It was obvious that something was drawing him to this young man. It felt as if his mind could only process one thing. *I have an idea.*

Hunter Grady

Hunter arrived at work earlier than usual. Saturday was usually a busy day. Even though his shift didn't start until ten a.m., he was there at nine a.m., hoping to pick up a little extra cash. He had just finished retying his loose shoe when his boss walked in.

"Good morning, sir," Hunter said.

"Hey, Hunter. You sure are early. You want to make some extra cash for tonight?"

"Extra cash? Absolutely. But what was that about tonight?"

"Oh. No one told you yet? You must have impressed someone. They left an invitation for you for dinner at Wagyu Steakhouse tonight. Nice work, dude!"

"Who is it from? I can't afford that. Jesus. It's like five hundred dollars a plate," Hunter said.

"I don't know what to tell you, man. Here is the invite." He handed Hunter the invitation.

Hunter eagerly flipped open the unsealed envelope. "You guys suck by the way. You read my mail… Assholes."

They chuckled.

Hunter,

Life is not about money. Life is about experiences. Please join me for dinner at Waygu tonight at 7:00 p.m. You are more like me than you know.

Sincerely,

Arthur

"Holy shit."

*

The day dragged on and on while Hunter's mind raced. *Why me? Why does he like ME?* This was of course impossible for Hunter to answer, but it didn't stop him from trying. All he could come up with was total shit, though. *I'm just a poor kid, and I can barely care for Mom and Rory. This is crazy. I don't even think I should go. What would I wear? Oh God.*

The clock ticked by as expected, however. And soon enough, it was six p.m. Now what? He had the jeans and T-shirt he had worn to work, but that wasn't really appropriate for such a high-end restaurant. *Well, I just hope I don't get laughed at.*

With that, Hunter rushed to the locker room. He slid off his work uniform and stood in front of the full-length mirror clad only in a tight jockstrap and black ankle socks. He gave his body a once-over, trying to see what anyone would want in someone like him.

His chest was firm, but thin. His arms and legs were skinny, but toned. Hunter did like his legs a little. They had seen a huge growth spurt since he got this job. Running all over this huge resort had really developed them. Maybe it was his abs. *Nope.* Just a flat belly, no abs. That left his ass and cock.

His ass was a voracious little pair of bubbles that even he was proud of. Hence the jock strap. And his cock was a solid seven inches hard, and thick too. He gave it a squeeze, causing it to thicken in the tight jock. But his cock didn't really matter. He was a bottom at heart, and his ass was where it was *really* at!

Hunter ran his hand over his ass-cheeks a few times as he glanced over his shoulder, watching intently in the mirror. It felt nice. He hoped someday a real man would want to touch him that way. To make him feel like he was worth something. One last stroke and he was done.

He needed to get dressed if he was going to meet Arthur at seven. He slid his tight-legged, skinny jeans on. Again, he paused to glance at himself. Next, he slid his tight T-shirt on. He thought he was *almost* cute with clothes on. Oh well. Off to dinner.

Arthur Westbrooke

Arthur had been nervously pacing in the private room. Wagyu Steakhouse had two main dining rooms and several private rooms. Arthur had insisted on a private room so that Hunter would not be ashamed of being seen eating with an old man.

The notion was probably ridiculous. Vegas was filled with preposterous people, and it was likely that no one would even notice. But he really wanted Hunter to be comfortable. And there was that thing about him ruining everything when he met people. Just like last night. Fewer witnesses are always better.

It was just after seven when Hunter arrived. The waiter escorted him into the small room.

"Hunter, thank you for coming. I wasn't sure you would," Arthur said.

"Actually, neither was I," Hunter replied.

"Please have a seat. First, let me apologize for my conduct last night. I was wrong to try to give you a kiss. I assumed you were gay and… I'm not one to know how to handle social situations, let alone be romantic."

"Well, you were right, I am gay. And you are very wrong. Look around us. Dim lights, candles, you in a suit and me in blue jeans. That's more romance than I have ever gotten. I feel pretty silly though. I am way underdressed. I guess that explains the private room."

"My God, I am so sorry. I hadn't thought," Arthur said. Before he had even finished speaking, he was on his feet. He removed the suit jacket and tie. He saw Hunter's eyes widen as he began to unbutton the dress shirt. He removed it and sat back down in just his white T-shirt.

"There. Again, I am so sorry, Hunter."

"Don't be sorry. Also that was not necessary, you know."

"I just want you to be comfortable."

"I am. Thank you. Although I have to admit, I was a little worried that your pants were next!" Hunter laughed.

"Ha! The waiter probably would not care much for that. Although… " Arthur leaned back in the chair and pretended to unbutton his pants. Hunter's face lit up with a smile. "You have a beautiful smile. It is so innocent. You are lucky."

"I'm lucky? Look at those arms! Arthur could see that Hunter was staring at his biceps. They were not huge, but big enough. He often got bored on his business trips and found the gym was a good place to burn off extra energy. Arthur blushed.

"No, really, it's true. Those things are hot! You must have guys jumping all over you," he said.

"Hardly. I'm… a bit awkward. Remember?"

"Listen," Hunter said. "I didn't leave last night because you tried to kiss me. I actually wanted that. I left because I… I have issues. Issues that I am sure you don't need. Not just stupid kid issues, but real adult issues."

"Hunter, if there is one thing you learn in life, it is that everyone has issues. You have to either accept that or check out of life!"

"Fair enough, but I might scare you with mine. Just a warning." He laughed.

"Please order whatever you want. Tonight is on me. No funny business. I promise."

The two went on and on over dinner. Each shared the battle scars of their lives. For some reason they both seemed at ease with each other. Like they were meant to be together. Arthur shared his issues with prostitutes and being older, and Hunter reciprocated, sharing his family issues and his time being a prostitute.

Neither was appalled by each other's stories. They actually drew closer. Each one now knew what the other had been through. As dinner concluded, both Hunter and he were red from laughter. Both had cried, just a little, but laughed a lot.

"Arthur, tonight has been the best night of my life. You are a wonderful man. I have never told anyone the things I told you, and it was easy to trust you. When are you leaving Las Vegas? I have to see you again before you go."

"I'm leaving on Monday. You better believe you have to see me again! I haven't had this much fun in forever. Are you off tomorrow?"

Hunter smirked. "I am."

"What is that look for?" Arthur asked.

"Let me show you."

He scooped a small bit of vanilla ice cream off his desert, walked to Arthur, stretched the neck of his T-shirt and dribbled it on Arthur's smooth chest. He gasped at the coolness.

"Oops." Hunter untucked and lifted Arthur's shirt before he sat on his lap. "I'll get that."

Hunter started his licking at Arthur's belly button and moved up until his warm, wet tongue met with the cool ice cream. A series of small moans escaped Arthur's lips. Licks turned to kisses and kisses turned to... more.

The waiter returned just as Hunter unfastened Arthur's belt. He jumped in surprise and excused himself. Hunter's beautiful smile returned and the two erupted into laughter. Hunter stood and adjusted his obviously hard manhood while Arthur did the same.

"Whoops." Arthur laughed. "Guess we're busted! Would you care to take this somewhere more private?"

"You couldn't stop me if you wanted to."

Arthur quickly paid the bill and the two rushed to his suite.

Hunter Grady

They burst through the door, feverishly smothering each other in hot, wet kisses. Guttural moans of pleasure escaped them both. Hunter literally ripped the shirt off Arthur, its white cotton shredding. He pushed Arthur backward onto the bed, kissing him down from his shoulders. He took each nipple into his mouth and sucked until it was rock hard.

Hunter kissed lower and lower until his tongue encircled Arthur's belly button. His hands traveled down his smooth, tan body until they reached his belt. Arthur begged for more as Hunter unbuckled it.

His kisses followed Arthur's beautiful V-shaped abdominals. First the right, then the left. He grasped Arthur's hardness and stroked it momentarily before kissing his way to the tip. He engulfed it over and over before Arthur flipped him over.

Hunter watched as his pants slid down over his hips and disappeared onto the floor. Arthur licked and kissed his way up the nineteen-year-old's body. Arthur buried his face in Hunters crotch, kissing all around the jock.

He felt Arthur guiding him over onto his stomach. He pulled the young man's hips toward himself, lifting his ass into the air. Arthur kissed up the back of his thighs and across the bubbly cheeks before he devoured the tight hole.

Hunter could feel Arthur's tongue exploring his depths for long periods of time before he had to surface for air. It was obvious that Arthur wanted to please him as he licked and stroked his flesh. It was too much.

"I need you inside me," Hunter said. "Please. I want to feel you inside me."

Arthur stood and lined his hardness up with Hunter's wet hole. Hunter moaned as he felt Arthur begin to slide into him. They locked into the throes of passionate lovemaking. Arthur took Hunter from behind for a short period before demanding to see his face.

They adjusted position, and now, face to face, kissed as Arthur thrust himself inside Hunter. They locked eyes. Hunter smiled between moans. This brought Arthur to the edge.

"I'm going to cum," he said and began to pull out of Hunter.

Hunter locked his legs behind Arthur's blocking him from pulling out.

"Don't go," he said and pulled him back inside.

Arthur's cock hardened and began to pulse with orgasmic delight. Hunter could feel him exploding deep inside. It was wonderful. It was the first time it had ever been like this and he didn't want it to end.

Hunter felt Arthur relax and collapse on top of him. The two kissed more and Hunter felt Arthur harden inside him.

"Again?" Hunter asked.

"Mmm."

The two made love late into the night until they were both too tired to go on, and sleep overtook them both.

*

Hunter returned home the next morning to a nervously awaiting mother.

"And where did you go last night? Hmmm?" she asked.

"I met someone," Hunter said.

"Ooh... Do tell," she said.

Hunter began to tell the story and was just about to the part at the steakhouse when the phone rang.

"Sit right there, mister. You don't get out of dishing just 'cuz the phone rang."

Hunter's mom retrieved the cordless phone from the pouch on her wheelchair and answered it.

"Hello? Yes, this is her. What?"

An unintelligible voice chattered on in the phone.

"How did this happen? You're sure it was for me? Oh, dear Lord... Thank you very much. Uh huh, bye bye," she said ending the call.

"Who was it?" Hunter asked.

"It was the bank. They said the house is paid off."

"What? How?"

"They said a gentlemen named Arthur Westbrooke called them and made the payment. I don't even know who that is."

"Oh my God. I do," Hunter said. "That's him, Mom. The

someone that I met. I had no idea he would do this. I have to call him."

Hunter pulled his cell phone from his pocket and dialed the Excelsior. "Please connect me with Suite 50-113," he said.

The hold music came on and Hunter paced impatiently. A woman returned to the line and explained that no one was available. He thanked her and hung up.

Just then the doorbell rang. Hunter bolted straight for it, nearly toppling his mom. He yanked the door open and there, in front of him, was Arthur. Hunter Leapt into his arms and smothered him with kisses.

"Hunter, may I come in?" he asked after the kissing subsided.

"Of course you can, don't be crazy."

"Mom, Mom, this is Arthur."

"It's a pleasure to meet you," she said, still in shock.

"How are you here? I mean how did you know where I lived? How did—"

Arthur cut him off mid-sentence, "There is a lot to explain, but there is little time to explain it in. To make a long story short, I received a call today that I must return home to deal with some work problems for a client. But there is another problem that I have to deal with first.

"There is no way I can leave here without you. I have never felt this way about anyone in my life. You are the one for me. I know it deep in my bones," Arthur explained.

"Are you sure that's not just arthritis?" Hunter asked through a huge grin.

"I'm fairly sure." He chuckled as Hunter's mom slapped him on the butt. "Now, I have another first class ticket in your name if you want to come," Arthur said.

"But I can't just leave my mom. She needs help here with the house and Rory. I really want to but—"

"Maybe I forgot to mention that a nurse from the hospital will be here in about an hour. There is a housekeeper due in first thing tomorrow and a part-time babysitter will be here to watch Rory. Oh, and I almost forgot. I took the liberty of ordering your mother a new electric wheelchair, and some new furniture will be delivered this afternoon. I hope you like blue, Ms. Grady. If not let me know and I'll have it changed out."

"But why? Why would you do all this," Hunter asked.

"Because, sometimes you meet someone so special that you can't ever let them go. Now, this trip is just for a few days, but I would like to eventually move your whole family to my home in Los Angeles if you'd come. I have a large casita for them," Arthur said.

"Oh, I don't know... I don't want to leave them behind," Hunter said, looking back at his mom.

"Don't be a fool Hunter. Go! I will be fine. Better than fine. GO!" she said. "Take a chance. There will always be Vegas."

7

LOVE AT THE LAS VEGAS BAKE OFF

C.H. Admirand

U.S. Marshal Ben Justiss stared across the lobby of the Excelsior Hotel. He had a bad feeling that hadn't gone away the closer he got to Las Vegas, and the woman he couldn't get off his mind.

One year, six months, and five days, and he could still see Peggy McCormack's sweet smile and taste her melt-in-your-mouth buttermilk pie. Damn sneaky tactic, overnighting him a fresh-baked pie from the diner she ran with her sister Kate in Apple Grove, Ohio.

He scanned the well-dressed crowd. It was going to be a logistical nightmare protecting Peggy during the First Las Vegas Bake-Off. He and his brother Matt had gone over the list of coordinators for the bake-off, the contestants, the media involved, and the hotel's support staff. They'd narrowed down the suspects to a handful since receiving the frantic call from her sister Kate and the heads-up from his cousin Patrick Garahan and his wife Grace Mulcahy Garahan—on speakerphone. Damn hard to concentrate with two people talking at the same damn time.

His gut burned. They were out of time. "Why didn't she call and ask for help?"

"Maybe she's still waiting for you to call and thank her for that pie." The deep chuckle from the other side of the potted palm separating him from his younger brother pissed him off.

"Didn't mean to say that out loud," Ben grumbled.

"Don't worry," his brother reassured him. "I don't think the guy in the tacky plaid slacks and hot pink golf shirt heard you."

Ben had spotted the guy in hot pink earlier. "This place is everything Tex's intel promised."

"I wonder if old Louie 'The Lip' LaFica is still kicking?"

Ben hadn't given the retired mobster who'd built the hotel in the 1960s a thought. His sole point of focus had been weeding out suspects and protecting Peggy McCormack from harm. "Wasn't there a rumor that he bought the farm back in 1975?"

"Unsubstantiated," his brother told him. "I'd like to have a talk with him."

"He'd have to be over one hundred years old," Ben said. "Might not survive interrogation."

"Maybe Tex's intel is off by a few years," his brother suggested.

"Even if it is," Ben said, "1960 is fifty-six years ago! Give or take five years either way he'd still be over ninety years old."

The lush potted palms and spiny cacti scattered throughout the lobby were a concern. But the number of additions to the hotel over the last twenty years had him wondering just how soon this job would be FUBAR.

"Have you spotted her yet?" Matt asked.

"Negative. I'll feel better when I see her."

Matt coughed to cover what sounded suspiciously like a laugh. "Sure thing, bro."

Ben knew his brother wasn't done ribbing him yet for not sending Peggy flowers. Matt sent women flowers for every occasion. "I was going to get around to thanking her."

"In this millennium?" Matt asked.

Before Ben could snarl out a reply, his brother rasped, "Main lobby doors. Tall, blond, and curvy."

Ben's gaze swung over to the doors. His gut twisted and his throat went dry. He'd forgotten how stunning Peggy McCormack was. "I should've sent flowers."

"You know it," Matt agreed. "What's the plan for contact?"

"According to the Ohio Garahans, this is a semi-hostile protection job."

"Wait, what—do Tom and John know?"

"Not sure. Peggy's sister Kate just called a few minutes ago," Ben said. "Peggy isn't taking the threats seriously." Watching the blond beauty striding from the doors to the long line at the reception desk, he frowned. "Kate warned she'd be difficult."

Ben moved closer to the front desk, while his brother circled around behind to make contact with the bodyguards they'd subcontracted for this job—two of their New York City cousins, Tom and John Garahan, both with the FDNY. They nodded as Matt walked past and touched a fingertip to his right ear.

"Got your ears on?"

"Roger Wilco," Tom answered, then said, "She looks different."

"She's not wearing jeans and her apron," Ben answered.

"Yo," John chimed in. "No ponytail."

"Yeah," Tom added. "She had long hair at Pat and Grace's wedding."

Ben's gut clenched, remembering a sky-blue dress swirling in the breeze and long blond hair shimmering in the sunlight. "Yeah."

Ben and his brother were the fourth generation of Justiss lawmen—U.S. Marshals. The code of honor and integrity was bone-deep and in their blood. It was similar to the cowboy code his Texas cousins lived by, and the brothers-in-fire code his New York City cousins lived by.

He moved into her line of sight and waited until she looked up. He touched the brim of his Stetson. "Miss McCormack."

Peggy's eyes widened. "I can't believe she called you."

"Right before Patrick and Grace called."

Her blue eyes flashed fire before narrowing. "I don't need a bodyguard. I need to win the bake-off."

He wanted to shake some sense into her. "Pretty descriptive threats."

She snorted and tossed her head, just like his favorite palomino filly at his folks' ranch... and just as feisty. "Bogus threats."

"Descriptive," he said again. "Right down to which bones they would break in your hands so you could never pick up a spoon or bowl again.""

He had the satisfaction of seeing her pale. *Not good enough.* He needed her scared enough to trust him and his team. "Kate forwarded another email a few minutes ago."

She was trying hard not to look interested. "I didn't receive any email this morning."

"It was sent to the main email address for the diner."

"And?"

He waited a beat and ground out, "They threatened to cut off your hands with a meat cleaver."

Her face lost every ounce of color. *Finally.* That got through to her.

But Peggy McCormack was a tough nut to crack. "Kate had no right hacking into my personal email, or to forward those emails to you."

"Your sister loves you and is smart enough to be scared for you."

She drew in a breath, giving him a chance to add, "Look, can we discuss this somewhere other than the middle of the lobby?"

"Where?" she asked, vibrating with outrage. "My room?"

He nodded. "It'd be more private."

"You had your chance, Marshal Justiss, and you flubbed it. I don't need you, and I sure as hell don't want you breathing down my neck right now. I need to focus." She pulled out her phone and ignored him.

If he wasn't so concerned that those threats were real, he might admire her damn-the-torpedoes attitude. "Stubborn," he mumbled, signaling for one of his cousins to shadow her. He was meeting the hotel manager in five and then doing a walk-through of the ballroom to see if they needed to make any changes to their protection detail. From the length of the line of people waiting to check in, he figured he had a little time before she would head up to her room.

A little while later, he strode out of the hotel manager's office, veering off toward the main ballroom. The Excelsior had been family-run since Louis "The Lip" LaFica first opened its doors, but so far he hadn't met any of the LaFicas. He wondered if the family made it a point to stay out of the public eye, or if it was just working for a living that they were avoiding.

"Heads up," Tom warned. "Line's moving."

Ben was about to head back to the reception area when John said, "Peggy's meeting with the bake-off coordinator, then will be registering for the bake-off. You've got time."

The main doors to the ballroom were locked, so he went around to the side. There was only one set of double doors and three other doors. Still, he covered all of the bases, asking and receiving approval from the manager to use the hotel's security tonight and over the next few days as needed.

Come hell or high water, he was going to keep that stubborn woman safe. A tall order, but he was up to the challenge and had his crack team as backup. If their Garahan cousins hadn't already had firefighting careers, he and his brother might have tried talking them into joining the U.S. Marshals.

He and Matt had started up a security company when the word came down about their suspensions on vague and unsubstantiated charges. But so far the jobs had been small compared to this venue. They'd been relieved when two of their cousins became available after being ordered to take some of the vacation time they'd been stockpiling.

With a tap to his earpiece, he communicated to his team, "Meeting in five... supply room by the freight elevator."

"I'll be meeting with the bake-off staff in fifteen minutes to get a final list of the contestants and their roommates," Ben said. "Tom, scope out the upper ballroom where the bake-off kitchen stations will be set up. John, check out all of the hotel bars. Matt secure the wing where Peggy's room is located."

"She's the last room in one of the new additions," Matt said. "The corridors and corners are poorly lit and don't show up on the hotel security cams."

"It might be our first security gig," Tom said, "but as long as one of you is either with Peggy or have eyes on her, what could possibly go wrong?"

The Justiss brothers shared a look. "Murphy's Law."

Tom grinned. "Anything that can go wrong.—"

"Will," his brother finished. "at the worst possible moment."

"Yeah," Matt said, "like rappelling off the Apple Grove water tower."

Ben chuckled. "We kicked your collective asses."

"Mike was just off the disabled list at his firehouse," Tom said.

"Pat was an ARI—alcohol related incident—waiting to happen," John reminded them.

Ben smiled. "It was his last night of freedom."

"You still haven't fessed up," Tom said.

"I still can't believe he let one of you goad him into that swan dive off the rail," John added.

Ben and Matt shared a look, and Ben said, "His cast looked great with his tux."

The Garahan brothers promised to settle the matter when the job was over and Peggy was safe. "She needs us," Tom said.

"Yeah," Matt agreed. "But I think the real problem is she doesn't want to want us—especially my brother."

"Shut up, Matt." Ben looked at his team. "Synchronize your watches."

"Spy-stuff." John grinned. "It's 14:55."

"Nope," Tom said. "14:57."

Matt looked at Ben, who said, "15:00 UTC/GMT."

Everyone reset their watches to match Ben's. "We meet back here at 18:00."

Chapter Two

"Hi, sis!"

Peggy McCormack frowned at her phone and the sound of her younger sister's voice. "You'll never guess who I ran into."

There was a telling pause before Kate said, "Don't be mad."

Peggy had to dig deep for a calm she didn't feel. "Why would I be mad, Katie? Because you went behind my back and called the one man I never wanted to see again?"

"I swear I—"

"Or because you hacked into my email?"

"I was looking for a supply order that might have gone to your email instead of the diner's main email account."

"And that makes it okay?" It was a good thing her sister was in Ohio.

"No," Kate whispered. "But Sis, an email came through the main account a little while ago… it scared me spitless."

The catch in her sister's voice cut through Peggy's anger. "Nothing is going to keep me from competing in this bake-off."

"That's why Grace convinced Mom and me to hire the Justiss brothers to act as your bodyguards."

"They brought two of their Garahan cousins."

"Tyler, Dylan, or Jesse?" Kate asked.

"Not the Texas Garahans," Peggy told her sister. "The New York Garahans."

"Even better," Kate sighed. "The FDNY Garahans. Who came? Mike, Tom, or John?"

"Tom and John."

Kate sighed. "Sorry I'm missing out on all of the fun."

"Someone has to run the diner."

She could hear heavy footsteps behind her. "Look, Kate, I've got to go. But I'll call you later."

"Okay, but you have to fill me in on tall, blond, and dreamy!"

Peggy agreed, then pressed the button for the elevator. The footsteps sounded closer. Was it someone connected to the threats?

Maybe it's Ben… the only man she'd ever sent a pie to…damn him for taking a little piece of her heart with him after Grace and Patrick's wedding. It was that damned crooked smile. Maybe it was his snug-fitting jeans… or the Stetson. She sighed, knowing it all was

109

all of the above, plus the way his hazel eyes lit up that time in the diner when she'd walked toward him with a pie in each hand.

"Hmmpf," she mumbled, "He was more interested in my pie."

"What was that about pie?" a familiar, deep voice called out from behind her.

She blew out a breath, relieved and, at the same time aggravated that it was Ben. She ran a hand through her close-cropped hair. Honey B. had cut it right before she left for the bake-off, and she wasn't used to the lack of ponytail yet.

"Miss McCormack." Ben sounded frustrated as he put his hand out to stop the elevator door from closing before he could get on.

What kind of man doesn't send a thank-you? She wondered. *The kind who isn't interested.*

"Peggy?"

She glared up at him. "You are in my personal space."

He didn't move an inch. "Yes, ma'am."

"And don't call me ma'am."

"All right, Miss McCormack."

"And don't call me miss," she told him. "It's Ms. McCormack to you."

"All right, Miz McCormack," he drawled. "About those email threats..."

The elevator chimed and she bolted as the doors opened. "Just some whacko trying to get me to back out of the bake-off."

"Will you?"

She didn't answer right away, or slow down until she'd reached the door to her room. "Not on your life."

"Can't or won't?" he asked, obviously hoping for clarification.

"Take your pick. I'm here to win."

"Why is winning so important?" He sounded genuinely interested.

"Time's up, Marshal Justiss. I've got to get ready for the cocktail reception." She opened her door, slipped in, and slammed it shut in his face. The grumbling coming from his side of the door had her smiling.

*

Peggy didn't understand why the man protecting her didn't even try to blend in. With his height and the white Stetson he wore, he was easy to pick out in a crowd.

A spurt of jealousy slithered up from the pit of her stomach as he smiled at a petite redhead. It would have to be her toughest competitor—Internet cooking sensation, Sofia Stellini. As if the woman needed the marshal to add to the group of men gathered around her. With her bright red hair, tiny black dress, and killer heels, the woman stood out among the more conservatively dressed black-clad women in the room.

Peggy made a mental note to ask her friend Rhonda at the Apple Grove Gazette to research the name of the idiot who had decreed that the little black dress was the only option to wear to a cocktail party. Her friend was great at digging up facts. Rhonda had been the one to find Ms. Stellini's Internet cooking videos. Cait, another friend, had been the one to update her hourly as to the number of views.

Sofia's red hair and bright green eyes distracted the viewer from the fact that her cooking skills weren't quite as dazzling as her cosmetically whitened smile. Peggy was positive she and Kate could cook rings around the woman—given the opportunity.

Ben's deep chuckle entwined with Sofia's husky laughter turning Peggy's stomach upside down. She'd wanted to ask Ben a couple of questions, but couldn't do that now. She did an about-face and walked over to the open bar, smiling at the bartender pouring a glass of red wine.

He nodded when the person in front of her gave him a tip, then smiled at her. "What can I get for you, pretty lady?"

She wasn't used to being the one served—she and her sister were the ones who did the serving at their diner. "I… uh…"

"The red's full-bodied," he said, not realizing Peggy was worried about a certain redhead currently captivating Marshal Justiss.

Peggy shook her head.

"Do you prefer a crisp white?"

Sofia's laughter drifted across the ballroom during a lull in conversation. "I'd like two-fingers of Jameson, please."

"On the rocks, coming up." He reached for a short, square glass.

A glance over her shoulder had Peggy digging deep not to fly across the room to yank Sofia's hair. "Up, please."

The bartender grinned at her. "Yes, ma'am."

"Don't call me ma'am," Peggy bit out. The man's eyes widened, and she realized how harsh she sounded "I'm sorry... Jason," she said, reading his name tag. "It's been a long day. Where I'm from, it's an insult to call a woman under the age of forty ma'am."

He chuckled as he poured. "You're making that up."

His laughter eased a bit of the tension shimmering in the ballroom air. "Nope. Are you from around here?"

"Yes, ma'am—um, miss. Just north of the city." As he handed her the glass, he asked, "You?"

She smiled. "Ohio."

"That's a world away from here."

"You can say that again." She smiled and left a tip on the top of the bar.

"I get off at midnight, if you'd like to go for a walk down the Strip. It's mighty pretty at night."

"Thank you." She beamed, "I'd love—"

"Miz McCormack seems to have forgotten her promise to discuss her latest culinary creation with me." Ben's voice rumbled from behind her. "I'm from *Sweet and Savory Magazine*." He extended his hand past her shoulder to shake the bartender's hand. "I couldn't help overhearing you're a native of Nevada. I'm from Colorado."

When she tried to step around Ben, he waylaid her with a hand to her elbow. "I'll be right with you, Miz McCormack, just need to grab a beer."

Biting her tongue to keep from telling Marshal Justiss what she thought of his ploy to keep her inside the hotel, she didn't see the waiter bearing a large tray of empty glasses headed her way.

The bartender called out a warning as the tray bumped against her shoulder knocking her into Ben. She nearly pitched to the floor, but Ben took the brunt of her weight, steadying her so she didn't fall. "Never let your guard down," he warned.

"How was I supposed to know that waiter was going to hit me with his tray?"

But Ben wasn't listening. He was speaking quietly into the headset she'd only just noticed. "Sorry," he apologized, turning back to her. "I missed that. What did you say?"

Unnerved by the possibility that someone had jostled her on purpose, reminded of the details of the last two threats she'd received, she answered, "It's not important."

Ben frowned at her, but didn't ask again. He was listening. "Roger that."

"I've got eyes and ears on you," he advised, keeping his voice pitched low. "You'll be safe until I get back."

She followed his line of sight and wanted to scream in frustration. Sofia smugly smiled in their direction as Ben walked toward her.

"I can take care of myself." Without a backward glance, she strode across the room, damning the marshal and his obvious attraction to Peggy's antithesis: the petite, slender redhead.

*

"Tex's intel ties Sofia Stellini to the LaFica crime family." Matt whistled. "Gotta be her."

"Checking it out now," Ben said, moving in Sofia's direction.

"Some guys have all the luck," Tom groaned.

"I need eyes and ears on Peggy," Ben rasped.

"On it," Matt said.

"Don't let her leave the hotel," Ben added.

*

Riding up to her floor, Peggy wondered why she couldn't accept the fact that Ben wasn't interested in her—or her blue-ribbon-winning pie. He hadn't called her like he promised after Grace and Patrick's wedding.

As she stepped off the elevator, the possibility that he never intended to see her again hit her right between the eyes. By the time she'd reached her door at the end of the long, dimly lit corridor, her head was pounding. Concentrating on unlocking and opening her door kept the tears at bay. She had a contest to prepare for and no time to wallow in self-pity just because a jerk of a lawman preferred tiny redheads to statuesque blonds.

"Yeah," she said out loud, feeling marginally better about herself and the situation. "Statuesque." Closing her door, she never even noticed the dark-haired man slipping through the exit door into the stairwell.

Chapter Three

Peggy moved around her kitchen station in a culinary dance all her own, captivating Ben. Scanning the perimeter, he watched the other competitors reaching for bowls and adding ingredients, but their movements weren't smooth and sure like Peggy's.

Focusing on the job and ignoring the twitch in the middle of his chest, Ben noticed movement at the back of the kitchen area. He was on his feet and halfway to the hallway when he heard Peggy yell.

"Hey, that's my grandmother's pastry cutter!"

Signaling to his brother to secure the hallway, Ben was a foot away when she grabbed her marble rolling pin and jabbed it beneath the thief's chin. "Give it back," she warned.

The dark-haired man snorted. "Or what, Blondie? You gonna clock me up with your rolling pin?"

Peggy's eyes narrowed, as she raised the rolling pin. Ben snagged it out of her hand and knocked the thief to his knees. "Move an inch, and I'll give it back to her."

"She's nothing!" the man cried. "A nobody!"

Since Peggy wasn't paying attention to the man or his continued taunts, Ben figured she was thinking about her pie crust.

"Did you call it in?"

"Las Vegas PD is sending a squad car," Tom answered.

"What about the hallway, Matt?"

"Last-minute delivery. Checks out."

"John?"

"Rear and side corridors clear."

Relief swept up from the soles of his feet. He'd lecture Peggy later about the dangers of clocking someone on the back of the head with her five-pound marble rolling pin. If she put her weight behind it, and hit him just right… He shook his head. *Later.* Time to remove the disturbance, so the competitors could get back to their stations.

The head of the committee reset the time clock as Ben hauled his captive through the ballroom doors. He should have realized that no one would have to carry in any weapons when the kitchen stations were loaded with them. Sharp knives, cleavers, nutcrackers and picks, and marble cutting boards and rolling pins.

He'd have to watch his step if he planned on getting to know the woman who'd use a rolling pin as a weapon to prevent the theft of a beat-up, half-moon-shaped tool with a wooden handle back. What did she call it again? Oh yeah, a pastry blender. "I thought you plugged blenders in," he mumbled, moving toward one of the side doors where hotel security had two men stationed to wait for the police to arrive.

"You use it to cut butter," his captive ground out. "Unless you are a peasant. Then you use shortening and cut it into a mixture of flour and salt."

"Doesn't sound very appetizing."

"Philistine!" the man grumbled. "Once the mixture is the right consistency, you add in water and behold!"

"Behold what?"

"Don't you know anything about pie crust?" the man asked.

Ben nodded. "Some taste better than others."

"My sister's is superior."

The hair on the back of Ben's neck stood up. "Your sister?"

"Sofia."

Ben's gut iced over as the pieces slipped into place. "It's Sofia Stellini!" he barked into his headset, turning the man over to the security guards. "All hands on deck—ballroom!" His heart pounded as he sprinted through the crowded lobby.

He hit the closed doors hard, ignoring the shards of pain tearing through his shoulder. Weapon drawn, he zeroed in on a dark-haired man who had to be a blood relative to the man he'd just carted outside.

He couldn't get off a clean shot off. Peggy was in the way. "Drop the knife!"

The man ignored him, raising the blade higher so the tip grazed her chin. The sight of her bleeding, galvanized Ben into action. "Close in," he said, never taking his eyes off the knife or the man wielding it. One of the scenarios they'd gone over was trapping the assailant using one of their great-grandfather's favorite methods—the square—where they'd close in on the perpetrator from all corners while the lawman on point would keep his weapon leveled on the outlaw.

Too bad, it wasn't the late 1870s, otherwise he could bring the Stellinis in, dead or alive. Right now, Ben was close to killing a man just to watch him bleed—a first because he'd always believed that the law would take care of punishing the criminals he and his brother brought in. The U.S. Marshals always got their man, but that man didn't always stay behind bars.

Ben intended to make sure this one did. "Miz McCormack," he said quietly, hoping to distract Stellini. "I never had a chance to thank you for that pie."

*

Peggy's eyes filled. "Too bad, Marshal Justiss. It's the only one I'll ever bake for you."

"Come on now, sweet thing," he soothed. "You know you've been wanting to send me another one, maybe a berry pie this time."

She sniffed. Stellini's grip loosened a hair's breadth, and she shifted slightly. "I'm not wasting any more of my grandma's super-secret pie crust or her recipes on the likes of you!"

"What's so secret about her pie crust?" Stellini asked, with a glance at his sister, the diminutive redhead at the station across the room. "You probably use shortening. Amateur!"

Peggy couldn't look Ben in the eye or run the risk of distracting him. Her chin burned where the knife had scraped across it, but she had no intention of letting the man cut her again. Digging deep for a casual tone, she asked, "If you wanted my recipe why didn't you just ask for it?"

He shifted his grip on the knife so he could tilt her face around when he asked, "And you'd tell me? Just like that?"

Praying that the knife wouldn't cut too deeply into her arm, she used a move she learned in self-defense class. Her hands shot up and out, breaking Stellini's hold.

White-hot pain sliced across her forearm. The room began to spin. A shot rang out, and Stellini fell against her, knocking the wind out of her as she hit the floor.

"Peggy?"

Pain kept time with the pounding of her heart as she struggled to catch her breath.

"That's it, sweet thing," Ben's deep voice crooned, keeping pressure on her arm. "Relax and just breathe," he repeated over and over until she could.

The EMTs were on the scene by the time she could breathe without sounding like a wounded bear. The gash on the outside of

116

her arm was going to make it hard to roll out any pie crust. She must have said that out loud, because the EMT paused to stare at her. "You're not going to be doing any cooking until they patch you back up in the ER."

Her breath snagged as her chest tightened. "Can't," she whispered. "Gotta compete."

Ben moved to stand beside the gurney she'd been strapped to. "First things first, Miz McCormack." A warm, callused hand grabbed hold of hers. "There will be other contests."

She shook her head at him. "I need to win this one." The realization that she wouldn't be able to bake her pie for the judges had tears gathering and slowly falling.

Ben reached over to capture a tear on the tip of his finger. "Why didn't you wait for me to make my move?"

She shrugged, then looked up. "You're mad at me?"

He frowned. "You didn't learn that move in any self-defense class."

"Yes," she insisted, "I did."

"Not when the assailant was holding a knife," he snarled. "You could have lost the use of that arm. Still might if he cut through enough tendons and nerves."

Her stomach heaved at the thought. She closed her eyes and began to breathe deeply. She didn't want to barf all over the man glaring daggers at her. When her stomach settled, she opened her eyes. "I did what I had to do."

"Funny thing about that," Ben said. "Stellini said the same thing when his sister came tearing across the room to smack him with her wooden cutting board."

"You're making that up," Peggy grumbled.

He shook his head. "You were too busy trying to catch your breath to notice."

"I thought they were working as a team against me."

"Not Sofia," he clarified. "Just her brothers, Fabio and Enzo."

"He's right, Ms. McCormack." The soft voice off to her left had her turning her head to see who it was.

"Then you didn't want my grandmother's pastry blender, or her pie crust recipe?"

Sofia tossed her head, and her long, fiery ponytail swished from one shoulder to the other. "I have my grandmother's recipe. She always used two knives to make her crust."

When Peggy noticed Ben staring at Sofia, a hitch beneath her heart sent the message to her aching head. Marshal Ben Justiss wasn't interested in Peggy or her pies. She was too tall, blond, and had given him nothing but grief since she'd overnighted that damn buttermilk pie to him.

Closing her eyes, she whispered, "Maybe we can have a pie bake-off of our own when my arm heals."

A finger poked into her good arm. "Here's my card. Email me when you get home. We can have the bake-off at your diner."

Peggy watched the set of Sofia's jaw as the woman continued, "We will ask this man to be the judge." Sofia whacked Ben on his shoulder, but didn't notice the color leach from his face. "*Si?*" Sofia asked.

"*Si*... er, yes," Peggy agreed, before adding, "Be prepared to lose."

Sofia's eyes flashed with anger. "Hah! You will be the one to lose," she promised, spinning on her heel, stalking back to her station.

"Where do you hurt, Ben?" Peggy asked loud enough for one of the EMTs to hear.

"I thought no one else was injured?" He scanned Ben from the top of his head to the toes of his boots.

"You've got a nasty greenish-gray cast to your face, Marshal," the other EMT said. "Sit down before you fall down."

Ben's brother and cousins must have been close enough to hear the conversation. They surrounded him, muscling him into the nearest chair.

"It's his right shoulder," his brother told the EMTs. Looking at Peggy, Matt added, "He dislocated it on assignment a couple of months ago."

Peggy realized that would have been around the time she'd sent Ben the pie.

"It'll be fine once it goes back into place. I can do it myself," Ben grumbled, but finally sat.

"Not on my watch," one of the EMTs told him, as the other one quickly immobilized Ben's injury.

"Damn," he groused, "didn't see that one coming."

His cousins were grinning at him, while his brother was shaking his head. "Wait until the guys at the department hear this."

"We're still on suspension, bro," Ben grumbled.

"Yeah, but I heard a rumor that Buzz Johnson has been under the microscope himself."

"Really?" Ben perked up at the news that their boss was being investigated. It was about time. Their boss had been gunning for the Justiss brothers since he'd discovered their family history as U.S. Marshals.

"Does that mean we can go back to work?" Matt asked.

Ben chuckled. "Thought that's what we were doing here." He glanced at Peggy. "All that's left to do here is the paperwork."

"After we go for a ride," one of the EMTs said.

Ben didn't let go of Peggy until they loaded her into the waiting ambulance. Muscling his way closer to her side, he grabbed hold of her hand again. "Peggy?"

She looked at him.

"I'm sorry, you were hurt."

She closed her eyes. Not what she'd thought he was going to say.

"If you had waited—" Ben started to say.

"Yeah, yeah," Peggy grumbled, interrupting him. "I wouldn't have gotten hurt. Well you know what?" she asked, glaring at him.

"What?"

"It hurt a hell of a lot more when you never called or emailed to tell me you received the pie I sent you."

"I was going to, but the assignment we were on went south and I dislocated my shoulder—"

"You couldn't pick up the phone?" Peggy couldn't believe how much Ben's excuses cut right through to the bone. He obviously didn't feel anything for her. As the siren wailed and the ambulance sped down the Strip to the hospital, she lectured herself to move on with her life and get over the man crowding too close to her injured arm.

When the ambulance hit a bump in the road, Ben jostled her arm. She gasped in pain. The EMT immediately moved Ben aside and checked her injury. "It's bleeding again," he said, reapplying pressure to her wound. "Hang in there. Another mile, and we'll be there."

Peggy wished she were back home in Apple Grove, surrounded by her family and friends. People who actually gave a damn about her, unlike the silent lawman riding in the back of the ambulance with her.

Her sister Kate was probably elbow-deep in lunch orders, trying to keep up without Peggy there to help. "I never should have entered that damned bake-off."

"Why did you?"

"Why do you care?"

Ben fell silent, as if he was trying to come up with a reason for asking. When he seemed incapable of conversation, she closed her eyes again, opening them when the ambulance came to a halt at the ER doors.

*

Two hours later she was patched up and medicated, with prescriptions for antibiotics and painkillers in her hand. How was she going to call for a cab when her phone and pocketbook were back at the hotel?

"Need a lift?"

Matt Justiss stood just inside the ER entrance, Stetson in his hands, waiting for her answer.

"What about your bone-headed brother?"

Matt grinned. "He'll have to call somebody else for a lift."

Peggy thought that sounded wonderful to her. "I'd appreciate it. I left my phone and wallet back at the hotel."

"Thought as much," Matt said, as they walked toward the door. "After we finished up the paperwork, I figured I'd head on over here to see if I could be of assistance."

Peggy was surprised to see the younger Justiss brother smiling at her. "What?"

"I can see why my brother's stuck on you."

That comment had her spinning around a little too quickly. "Are you nuts? He hates me."

Matt's smile broadened. "Big-time stuck on you." He held out his arm. "Just lean on me, if you need to, Ms. McCormack."

He nodded to a shiny black, extended cab Ford F-250. "Let me help you."

Once she was sitting on the bench seat, she started to feel guilty. "Maybe you should see if Ben is ready to go."

Matt cheerfully answered, "He only drives. Hates to ride shotgun."

Peggy sighed. "What about the backseat?"

"He'd have to be drunk or unconscious to ride in the back."

"What about the truck bed?"

Matt's crack of laughter filled the cab and lightened her heart. As he put the truck in gear and eased the clutch out, she heard somebody yell, "Where the hell are you going with my truck?"

She looked out the window and saw a red-faced Ben vibrating with anger trying to chase after them. "Matt, stop!"

Matt shrugged, but didn't stop.

"He might trip and fall on his bad shoulder," Peggy rasped.

Matt slowed down. "And that would bother you? I thought you didn't like my brother."

"I wish I didn't," she whispered.

Matt parked the truck and got out.

"Where are you going?" Peggy asked. "I can't shift with all these stitches in my arm."

Ben opened the driver's door and got in. "My truck," Ben snapped out, "I'm driving."

Peggy was about to argue when she noticed the sling. "You can't shift with that arm."

Matt got in behind her and leaned forward. "It'll take teamwork, Peggy. He'll work the clutch, and you shift with your left hand."

"Remind me to punch him when my shoulder feels better."

Peggy was about to say something when Ben grumbled, "Pay attention. I'm clutching here."

Matt laughed. "My brother's a good team player," he told her. "He just sucks at relationships."

Ben growled, but was concentrating on working the clutch without also shifting. "Damn hard to do. Wait, I'll pull over and take this sling off."

"No!" Peggy said, moving the gearshift when he depressed the clutch again. "I've got it. Quit stomping so fast on the clutch and my shifting will be smoother."

Ben turned to glare at her, and to her surprise, his glare softened to a look of admiration.

"What?"

"Told ya," Matt called from the backseat. "Big-time stuck!"

"Hmmpf." Peggy didn't believe it for one minute.

"He's right," Ben rumbled.

For a heartbeat, Peggy thought he was going to tell her he cared.

"I really suck at relationships."

Peggy figured she'd have gray hair before the frustrating man sitting next to her admitted to having feelings for her. "Well you suck at common courtesy too."

He didn't look away from the road ahead of them. "Clutching here."

Peeved at the thick-headed man, Peggy snapped, "Shifting here."

Matt laughed again and Ben swerved to the side of the road. "Shut up, Matt!" he hollered over his shoulder. He depressed the clutch and held it to the floor, coasting to a stop.

"Where are you going?" she asked when Ben turned the truck off and got out. He didn't answer. She turned around and asked Matt, "Where is he going?"

Her door swung open wide, and Ben reached inside and grabbed hold of her left hand. With a yank, she was plastered to his chest. She tried to wiggle out of his grasp, but bumped her arm and hissed out a breath.

"Easy," Ben soothed. "You'll hurt yourself."

"Yeah?" Peggy said. "Well, you've already done that and more, cowboy. I can walk back to the hotel from here."

Ben tightened his grip. "No."

She narrowed her gaze and glared up at him.

He didn't move, didn't blink.

"What now?" she demanded, irritated beyond belief when his gaze shifted down to her lips and his eyes darkened to a deep blue. "Whatever you're thinking, you can forget about it." She struggled but couldn't break the hold he had on her.

"I've been wondering if you taste as sweet as your pie."

"You are not going to kiss me!"

He smiled and the knots in her chest eased. "Wanna bet?"

The catcalls coming from inside the truck sounded farther away with each soft press of his lips against hers. "Well I'll be," he said, easing back and smiling down at her.

Peggy couldn't feel the top of her head and wasn't sure her feet were still on the ground when Ben bent his head to kiss her again. "You taste sweeter than your buttermilk pie."

"That's not much of a compliment." She tried to push away from him.

He didn't budge. "I wonder if you're as delicate as your pie crust."

Peggy knew she was in way over her head.

"You two want to get in before that policeman over there arrests you two for disturbing the peace?"

Ben laughed and opened the back door, and helped Peggy inside, sliding in next to her. "To the hotel, bro. Miz McCormack and I have some catching up to do."

"Just because I let you kiss me doesn't mean I'm letting you do more than that."

The desire swirling in the depths of Ben's hazel eyes had her as breathless as his kisses.

"Wanna bet?"

"I thought you didn't gamble?"

"I'm not the one gambling, you are."

Peggy laughed. He was making her crazy. She could use some crazy in her life. "I never gamble on a sure thing."

He smiled down at her. "I was stuck on you from the minute I walked through the door to the Apple Grove Diner and you smiled at me."

"You were hooked on my pie."

He shook his head and tilted her chin up with the tip of his finger. "Nope. On you, Peggy McCormack." His mouth hovered a breath away from hers. "Kiss me back, sweet thing."

And she did.

8

FINDING A HERO

Christina Skye

Her room had been empty when she left.

Maddie Munro was dead certain of that.

Now someone was inside. A man.

She stood frozen, listening to low muttered laughter drift down the hall from the bedroom.

Then she saw her open bathroom door.

A naked man, given one quick glimpse through the shadowed doorway. He was stretched out in her bathtub, completely at home.

Maddie heard the sound of water and a low male voice, talking on a phone. Silently, she moved back out to the hall. She looked at her room card and the number she had scribbled down.

Room 301.

The gold letters gleamed on her door.

Her room alright.

What was she supposed to do now? Call security? Scream?

Sighing, she stepped inside and pocketed her card.

It was a beautiful suite in the Excelsior Hotel with floor to ceiling glass windows that overlooked the strip. If she stood just right, she could see the spectacular fountain and music shows like clockwork at the Bellagio.

The suite was way above her pay grade. But then Maddie wasn't paying. Otherwise, she'd be camped out at the cheapest local branch of the YWCA.

But this was a job, and Maddie's employer happened to be a secret unit of the US government. And for *her* kind of skills they paid very well indeed.

Water slapped quietly from the end of the hall.

She was still trying to decide whether she should go inside and confront the man or simply call security, when she heard the man's voice rise. The words were rougher now. He was speaking Russian.

No, not Russian, she decided. It sounded like a dialect from Ukraine, near the Black Sea. She collected odd information like that. Languages happened to be a passion of hers.

She tilted her head and listened to the man sing. Scraps of melody teased her memory.

She had it now. It was a particular song that was sung by the crime syndicates around Odessa. The words had something to do with how to treat a woman to keep her quiet.

The pig.

The creepy, arrogant pig.

Maddie scowled.

He really thought he could crash her room and sing creepy, woman-hating songs? Wait until the hotel management heard about it.

Water splashed hard. She heard a door open. A man's voice boomed out and feet scuffed over carpet. By instinct, Maddie slipped into the nearby closet. She didn't want a scene just yet. Through the louvers at the bottom of the door she watched a pair of bare feet move past. Water splashed on the carpet and then a big hotel towel dropped to the floor.

Holy grapeshot.

She shrank back, listening as he placed a call and spoke quickly. It was more of the Black Sea dialect. She couldn't follow any of it.

Maddie realized that she was supposed to meet her boss downstairs in exactly twelve minutes. They had been assigned to run security for a high-profile wedding at the hotel, a favor called in by a senator who was an old friend of her boss.

The old boy's network. Frankly, the whole idea made Maddie sick. If she had a problem, she didn't have anyone to call for a "Get out of Jail Free" card. Not one. Life was tough, but did you hear her complaining?

She sniffed, angry at the way this whole trip had gone south from the moment she'd left DC.

Down the hall she heard the man stop and turn slowly.

Okay, big mistake sniffing. She hadn't realized he was so close.

She waited silently, her shoulders stiff with tension while long seconds trailed past.

The feet turned and moved on down the hall.

When she was sure he was gone, Maddie drew a slow breath and punched a brief text to her boss.

May be late. Someone here in my room. You send anyone up?

She had switched the phone to silent mode and waited impatiently for a reply.

Not me.
Will check with front desk.
Better be careful.

Big help he was. Damned right, she'd be careful.

A door closed. Maddie could tell it was the bedroom at the end of the hall. She opened the closet slowly, checking the distance to the front door. She could make it without being discovered.

Time to move.

Except she couldn't leave her laptop, not the gleaming silver model with all its sweet new technology crammed under the cover.

An arm locked over her shoulders. Hard fingers closed over her throat.

Maddie kicked out wildly, feeling a tough, damp male body behind her.

Before she could spit out a scream, darkness gripped her, pulling her down in a cold, sickening rush.

Chapter Two

Gabriel Ross stared down at the figure stretched out unconscious on his couch. The woman was so small. So damned fragile, despite the spiky purple hair and the single Celtic cross earring.

He hadn't meant to put her out. Hell, he hadn't even known she was in the suite. He'd acted by pure instinct. And all his chokeholds were meant for thugs who weighed about 200 pounds more than this woman did.

But there was no reason for her to be in his room. He could have put it down to a simple mistake by the hotel computers, but Gabriel made it a firm rule never to trust in simple mistakes.

Because generally they hid something really bad.

So he came back to question one. Why in the hell was she here?

He circled the couch and grabbed his phone, scowling. "Yeah, it's Ross. Better get up here. She's coming around any second."

He jerked on his clothes, all the time keeping an eye on the couch.

This was supposed to be a simple two-day security operation. Spoiled senator's daughter marries the slick young son of a Silicon Valley software billionaire, while an adoring press crowds close. But it was starting to look as if the operation had a leak on the inside, somewhere in the hotel administration. Someone wanted to create confusion, throw up smokescreens and buy time for an unknown entity to crash the wedding.

There had already been blackmail threats from the Russian mob. Or the Miami Haitian mob or the Jamaican mob. Right now the source was unknown. And Gabriel hated wasting precious time here when he should be out cornering leads.

On the couch the girl stirred. Her hand slid over her throat. She gave a low, harsh cough. A second later she shot to her feet.

Her eyes held a snarl. "Get away from me, you creep."

But now she was holding out a small piece of metal, Gabriel saw. It looked like a cigarette lighter, but he was pretty sure it was something else entirely.

"Just so you know, this isn't Mace. It's far worse." She waved the little silver square. "If you don't get back, you're going to be blind for life."

Gabriel almost believed her. She seemed tough for someone so young. How old was she anyway? Seventeen? Eighteen tops?

He shrugged away the thought. All that mattered was why she was in his room.

He raised one hand in a slow gesture meant to soothe. "Calm down. I can explain this." Like hell, he could. "I didn't mean to put you under. You caught me by surprise, that's all. Why don't you put down the lighter so we can talk."

"I told you, it's not a lighter. And there's no point in talking. So get into the closet. Do it *now.*"

"Maybe you could calm down."

"Maybe you could kiss my ashes." The woman glared, circling behind him. "I'll calm down when I see you inside that closet with the door locked. Now get your hands up in the air."

Gabriel hid a smile as he turned around. She had a lot of guts, he'd say that. She couldn't possibly know how highly he was trained. He could have her flat on the ground, wrists and legs bound in less than three seconds without making any noise. It was what he did.

And he was damned good at his job.

"Sure." He shrugged, smiling as if embarrassed. *Mr. Nice Guy.* "Fine. I'll go. Whatever you say."

He walked to the closet and stepped inside. It still held her scent. Cinnamon. Bubble gum.

What a ridiculous mess.

At the back of the closet, he turned, hands still raised. "Can I make a phone call to the front desk?"

"I'll make the calls here, amigo."

"You still think that I want to hurt you?" He shook his head and moved slowly toward her. "That's nuts. I don't even know you."

"Stay *back.*" She snapped at the air with the not-lighter.

Gabriel wasn't really worried. Even if the woman did figure how to engage the heavy latch on the lower edge of the closet door, he'd be free in seconds. The wooden frame was remarkably flimsy. He had assessed that as soon as he entered the room, as part of his initial security check.

What did bother him was her attitude. She was clearly upset. She considered she had every right to be in the room. Since she didn't appear to be drunk or under the influence of drugs, there was no reason for her to mistake the room number.

So why was she here?

Not your problem.

He would leave it to the on-site liaison to deal with. His local contact should be here any minute. There were hotel room blueprints to run, guest background checks to complete, and personnel records to assess. And they only had twenty-four hours until the big fiasco wedding took place.

Gabriel didn't get the whole wedding thing. He certainly wouldn't have a noisy, orchestrated pageant like this and he wouldn't choose a high profile place like the Excelsior. Not that he'd ever found the right woman. Probably he never would. He simply wasn't built for loyalty and long-term commitment.

Except to the secret brotherhood who employed him.

Given the 24/7 relentless demands of his job, it was just as well that he didn't have a commitment gene, Gabriel thought grimly.

He heard something slide under the slats at the bottom of the door. Metal clanged outside. A silver pipe twisted around the edge of the door.

Maybe the woman wasn't so slow after all. It might take him three minutes rather than thirty seconds to break out.

Footsteps moved past the doorway. He heard her angry voice trail away down the hall toward the bedroom.

"That's right. A man. A big nasty man. He's here in my room."

Nasty? Him?

Maybe she had a point, Gabriel thought. He had put her out cold.

"Hell, I don't know. Six-foot something. Sandy blond hair."

Sandy? There was nothing wrong with his hair.

"Muscles. Yeah, I guess he seems fairly fit."

Fairly?

Gabriel leaned closer, trying to hear the muffled words from the bedroom. "Well he's locked in the closet, so you'd better get up here. And why you're at it, see who issued his room card. Yes, of course I've got my laptop. Assuming the big goon didn't steal it while I was gone."

Goon?

Gabriel reached into his pocket for his phone, punched in a code, and watched room numbers shoot up. He scanned the name list of everyone currently staying at the Excelsior Hotel.

There she was.

301. Madison Munro.

No sign of his name anywhere.

He ran another search and got the same results. Someone had shifted the room assignments.

Frowning, he rubbed his neck. He had been running personnel checks when he had stopped to wash off the dust of seventy-two straight hours of inflight travel. He had already turned up irregularities in seventeen hotel employees, the kind of things that triggered further search. Calling out sick meant a break in pattern, and you always tracked whereabouts, large deposits of money, and connections with suspicious or hostile organizations.

Gabriel highlighted five names. These were his target employees, all returning to the afternoon shift. Damn it, he had work to do.

He put his shoulder to the door and shoved.

Wood creaked. Something heavy and metal banged outside near the floor. He took a step back, leaned in and rammed the door with full force. Metal twisted and two wood slats shattered.

He exploded through the newly made hole.

The woman with the purple hair was ready for him.

The silver not-Mace device was held out in front of her as she faced him from the end of the hall.

"Put it down, Madison. I don't want to hurt you."

"What makes you think that's my name?"

She frowned and her hands shook slightly, betraying the strength of her voice.

"We both know the answer. You're Madison Munro. And we can figure this out. But I'm running out of patience." Gabriel moved toward her.

"Stay back. I'll use this stuff, I mean it."

He shook his head and kept walking.

Behind him the room bell chimed. That had to be his local contact.

About freaking time.

"I'm answering that," he said gruffly.

"Get back in the closet. I'll handle the door." The woman who said she was not Madison Munro frowned as it became obvious that the closet would hold no one until the big hole was repaired. As she hesitated, Gabriel swung around and flicked open the door.

The man outside was tall and rugged, and his mahogany features were just the way Gabriel remembered. The man even made the hotel room service uniform look good.

"What the hell is going on in here?"

"Why don't you tell me," Gabriel snapped. "We've got a problem. I checked the hotel room list, and her name is on it. 301. Someone switched things around."

Then something heavy struck him in the back of the neck. He cursed as another blow hit his left shoulder.

Izzy Teague, ex-DEA agent and high-level government operative, shoved a metal room service table through the door and pinned the struggling woman with the spiky purple hair against the wall. "Stand down, Maddie. Gabriel is one of ours."

"Ours? This creep?" She glared at Gabriel. "I don't buy it. He was singing creepy Russian mafia songs."

How had she known that? Gabriel hadn't been aware of the singing himself, but after he left deep cover it always took him a few days to wind down.

"Why didn't you warn me he would be here in the room?"

"Because I didn't know. I'll go check it out if you'd stop waving that new protection spray around." Izzy Teague tossed a backpack on the table and opened Maddie's laptop. "Sit down. I need you to run a personnel check on someone at the hotel."

"Would someone tell me what the hell is going on?" Gabriel growled. He watched the woman called Maddie manipulate the keyboard of what appeared to be the very latest government issue hardware. Her laptop was lightning fast and amped up with major encryption protocols. Gabriel had only seen one other with this kind of hardware.

So she had to be very good at her job.

But he didn't like being ignored, not after working three hours on his own data search. "I have the hotel list narrowed down to five targets, Teague."

"Good. Show me later." Teague leaned over Maddie as she worked, watching data stream past. "Get me a complete background on the first name on that list. Full stats and employment. Friends, family, arrests. The whole gorilla." He glanced at his watch and frowned. "And make it fast because the first wedding guests have begun to arrive."

Chapter Three

Sometimes Maddie loved her job.

Sometimes working for the government was a real ray of sunshine in a very dark world.

She rolled up her sleeves with a flourish. "Gimme the whole name, boss."

"I *hate* it when you call me that."

Maddie hid a smile. Of course she knew that. And it was why she did it.

"McNamara. Timothy J." Izzy Teague spelled it out and watched Maddie type. "He works in hotel beverage services."

"Date of birth?"

Izzy rattled off the numbers.

"Okay. Let's see what we've got for this bad boy." Maddie studied the scrolling text as she typed quickly. Personnel checks were no challenge at all. She could run them in her sleep.

"Roommate employed in the hotel laundry. Both of them are out sick today. Bought a new car last month. Nice one. Lexus. Roommate's bank account last month was $325.17. Now it's…"

Maddie gave a little whistle. "$492,712. I'd say that's bingo."

"I could have told you about the bank account. About the new car too," the man behind Maddie's chair said flatly.

"I needed redundancy of search, Gabriel. You know how it works." Government operative and ex-DEA agent Izzy Teague gave a quick nod at Gabriel. "You two stay at this. I'm checking out food services and the laundry. I want to see McNamara's work locker and find out what his co-workers have to say about both men. Meanwhile, I want you running deep, Maddie. I need prior addresses. Phone numbers, friends, family. Travel and buying habits." He glanced at his watch. "After I finish downstairs, I'm checking their apartment. I've got a dog waiting out in the van."

Dogs? Maddie loved it when they used the search dogs. It was so cool to watch the big, tough animals run down a scent. Those trained noses were awesome in action. "B and E? I could help you with that," she said brightly.

"Stand down, Einstein. I'll handle the physical evidence search. I don't need to remind you that we only have twenty-three hours until the *Bridal March* begins. The Senator will be on site in about six hours."

Maddie's stomach rumbled.

Izzy frowned. "No breakfast? Sorry about that. I know I promised you a few hours off. Get something to eat here in the room. Call room service."

"Don't worry about me. I'll be fine, boss."

"I'll order something for you anyway. And remember to eat what they bring up. Don't get lost in program code and coffee fumes. I need you in top shape." Izzy grabbed his backpack and shared a look with the man called Gabriel. "Keep an eye on her until I get back, Gabe."

The door closed quietly behind him.

Chapter Four

For top shape, Maddie needed energy.

Energy as in mega caffeine.

An oil tanker full of coffee would do nicely. Since the tanker was out, she'd settle for downing it by the pot.

But the nearest good coffee shop with a roaster was three miles away, down the strip. And that was just plain unfair.

The one thing her new job had afforded her was the ability to indulge in her particular vice for artisanal, single origin coffee. She would have given her entire bank account for a cup now.

Given that her bank account currently totaled $73.21, it would be worth the cost.

But there was no point dreaming about the impossible. She glared at the man called Gabriel, stalked across the room, grabbed her backpack for fresh bubblegum and then went to work.

Old personnel files shot over the page. Security profiles from DC appeared next.

One decent cup of coffee would have helped so much.

Air brushed her neck. Rich aromas danced across her nose.

Coffee.

Her eyes fluttered. "Is that what I think it is?" Maddie took a long, savoring breath.

"Probably." The man set a cup down beside her hand. "Looks like you could use this while you wait for room service. Just don't gulp it. This is the really good stuff, and it's all I have left."

She took a careful sniff.

South America.

Single varietal.

She took another smell, letting the smoky scent roll over her nose. "Yellow Bourbon varietal. Brazil. Fazenda de Ines." She closed her eyes, following the impressions on the hot steam. She didn't take her coffee lightly, not a bit. It was about the only indulgence Maddie allowed herself these days.

"These beans are a little old. Probably a week past their prime. Not that I'm complaining. I haven't had anything half this good since I left my apartment in DC."

The man stared at her. He was wearing a dark green sweater now. It picked up the deep, restless color of his eyes. "You picked all that up from *one* smell?"

Maddie flushed, feeling a little embarrassed. But proud too. She knew her coffee, okay? She was allowed to be proud about that. "It's just this thing I do. Not brain surgery, you know."

He was still staring at her. "From one smell you could dig up all that?"

She shrugged and reached for the coffee. Dark, moody enchantment played over her tongue. Light citrus and clove layers mingled and danced. The coffee tasted even better than it smelled.

Orgasm in a cup.

Maddie blew out a little breath. Where had that thought come from?

When the man with the sandy hair moved in closer, she picked up his smell too. Citrus and lime. Smoke. Something else she couldn't name.

It irritated her that she wanted to try.

Because his scent was almost as tantalizing as the coffee.

She shot to her feet. "This stuff is awesome. I mean, wow. But I'd better get back to these personnel files."

He leaned over her shoulder, and she was hit with the smoky male scent all over again. "No need to get jumpy."

Who was jumpy?

Maddie glared at him as he ran a finger down her laptop screen until he found one particular name. "My intel says that McNamara has some serious connections in Miami. He also has a grudge against the senator. Seems his cousin was arrested for threatening letters after a little matter of $50,000 in unpaid IRS bills two years ago. The senator refused to act in the family's behalf. Our man McNamara was not a happy taxpayer after that."

"I'll check his recent travel patterns." Maddie figured it would take her about four minutes to do that.

She shoved up your sleeves and then stretched slowly. Her stomach growled, and the old twinge in her shoulder began to act up again.

Where in Sam Hill was room service when you needed them? Whatever.

The man stared at her arm. "Looks like your shoulder hurts. An old accident?"

He'd noticed that? Most people paid no attention to Maddie. She

136

liked it that way, staying anonymous and sliding under the radar. People asked too many questions and made too many stupid assumptions.

"So what was it, accident or injury?"

She rolled her shoulders carefully and frowned. "Yes."

"Very funny. Accident?"

"Kind of."

"Don't overwhelm me with medical facts here."

"I don't intend to."

The truth was, the injury had come several months before. Maddie had been on a job in London. Her first work for the government, in fact. She'd been amped up, determined to impress her boss. Then the proverbial stuff hit the fan. Maddie was still trying to process that trifecta of horribleness.

But some good stuff had come out of it. Like the amazing man she had met in a London cemetery. Really. He had walked out of the foggy night and pulled her down into an open crypt, nearly giving her cardiac arrest.

She still smiled at the thought.

The really weird part was that the rugged, gorgeous man was apparently *bound* to her. By some kind of very old vows. Maddie was trying to figure out the whole relationship thing, since she had nada experience with relationships before this.

Unfortunately, everything had gotten complicated fast. Lately her rugged stranger was acting moody whenever they talked. And he wouldn't answer her direct questions.

It made Maddie *crazy*.

Given the fact that there were a set of very nasty demon-things following him through a changing time warp, he had reason to be distracted.

But good luck explaining *that* to anyone.

Behind her the man called Gabriel donned a silver earbud and walked to the window. He looked down and gave a two-finger wave to someone Maddie couldn't see.

A contact down on the street. Tracking their hotel target, probably.

Maddie frowned as the tall man listened and then spoke quietly into the small mic.

This time he spoke in Gaelic. Fast and fluent. Who was he?

None of your business, Maddie girl. Get back to your spread sheets. Sooner you're done, sooner you'll be back home, savoring some amazing coffee. Maybe you'll score a trip to England, and when you get there, Lyon might be happy to see you. Less distracted, as if he wasn't planning something dangerous that he didn't want you to know about.

Maddie shivered, feeling a sense of danger that she couldn't place.

"Cold?"

"I'm just fine."

The man shrugged and turned back to the window.

But when she looked down, a small glow played around her hands, swirling and soft, part of a strange new skill that Maddie was still fighting.

Twisting and alive, the lights danced over her arm in slow spirals.

The *marks* were back. The ones Maddie didn't want and didn't understand. And they carried a warning.

Chapter Five

The man named Gabriel kept the coffee coming while Maddie worked, pulling up rental car records and prior employment for their target. Timothy McNamara had been a busy man, traveling all over the Southwest and California in the last six months. He had used an alias, of course. It had taken Maddie all of two minutes to crack that.

She hunched over the laptop, frowning, fingers racing across the keyboard. Thankfully the glow-thing had settled down. No more marks that played over her hands. Maddie definitely didn't want to explain *that* to anyone.

"What do you think he's up to?"

Maddie jumped as Gabriel moved up behind her. She hadn't even felt the air stir. "Stop that. It's creepy how you make no noise." Her skin tingled as he reached over her shoulder.

"Sorry. Habit." He studied the screen. "What's this?"

"Rental car pattern for McNamara's roommate named Kade. About thirty cities in the last year."

Gabriel rubbed his neck and glanced off into space. "That's interesting."

"What is it?"

"My guess is military bases. Thirty-two of them, spread out all over the southwest and California." He turned back to the laptop, frowning. "Tucson. Glendale. Flagstaff, Arizona. Davis Air Force Base. Luke AFB. Camp Navajo Army Base. California locations here too. Edwards. Pendleton. Vandenberg."

He rattled off more names, and Maddie was stunned. Clearly he was right. Why hadn't she seen that pattern herself? "What happens next?"

"I'll call it in. Get me a list of dates crosslinked to each location. Can you do that fast?"

"Piece of cake. Except I could really use some coffee."

Gabriel smiled and shook his head. "I can see Izzy was right about you. But you need to eat. Here's a protein bar. Field rations, so it isn't gourmet, but it gets the job done. Perfect blend of protein and carbs for energy efficiency."

Maddie took a bite and frowned. "Fine. That's it for the protein. How about more coffee?"

"Eat it all, Einstein. Then we'll see about coffee."

She shrugged and finished the bland bar, feeling better immediately. Her stomach stopped growling too. The fact was that Izzy Teague called her an adrenaline junkie, and Maddie had to admit that he was right. That particular tendency had gotten her into trouble far too often, starting with the time that she and her friends had hacked into the Department of Defense mainframe computers when Maddie was just fourteen.

Seriously lame.

Remembering all that made her feel stupid and childish, so she swung back to work. Work was the one thing that made her feel balanced. Useful. Not a total outsider.

Maddie felt Gabriel behind her, and his presence made her restless. She reached past him, grabbing for the last of her coffee, but her big silver earring snagged on the edge of his sweater. She muttered in pain, her hand clenched in surprise. The coffee cup slipped through her trembling fingers.

Gabriel's hand shot out.

The cup was retrieved in midair before it splashed hot coffee all over Maddie's chest and hands. The movement had been a blur, completely silent.

She blew out a breath. "Thanks. That was definitely going to hurt."

"No problem."

He leaned down slowly, tracing a line along Maddie's wrists. Frowning as if he couldn't figure something out. "Why don't you explain to me about these."

"They're usually called hands."

"I'm talking about the other thing. The lights. The ones that move over your arms. I saw them."

Maddie sucked in a breath. She couldn't talk about this. Not to anyone but Lyon. And Lyon was all the way across the ocean on a different continent.

"You need glasses, Gabriel. These are hands and nothing else."

He reached around her shoulder, gently freeing the earring from the wool sleeve of his sweater. "My eyes are fine, Maddie." He turned her wrist over slowly and traced the soft skin.

His touch made her breath catch. Something warm and restless began to hum down into her chest.

"How old are you anyway?" he murmured. His hand slid over

her wrist, smoothing it as if he had nothing else to do in the world. As if he enjoyed touching her and wouldn't mind doing more of it. "Seventeen? Eighteen?"

She cleared her throat and pulled away. "I'm old enough to know that we both need to get back to work."

"Not quite yet," he murmured. "You've got dirt on your cheek."

"Where?" Maddie rubbed her face, frowning.

"Here." Gabriel brushed a line along her chin. "It's been there ever since I broke out of the closet. You must have done it when you locked me inside." He frowned, anchoring her face with strong fingers. His touch was impossibly light, Maddie thought.

Gentle.

As if she mattered in a way he couldn't figure out.

Make that two of them.

"Gabriel, I don't think—"

And then his mouth brushed hers. The heat and strength and smoky smell of his skin struck her like a bolt of lightning, tangling her nerves, snapping along her senses. Maddie's chest seemed to be too tight. She couldn't get enough air to breathe.

And she wanted more.

She closed her eyes, leaning into his touch, feeling the snap of heat grow.

Gabriel muttered something in Gaelic. His mouth hardened, and he pulled her against him, dropping his arm around her waist until they were locked in dizzy.

Maddie felt as if she was drinking sunlight, spinning into space. It was crazy and scary.

Gabriel took a harsh breath. Then he pulled away. His fingers feathered over her cheek, tightened, and fell to his side.

His eyes burned over her. Measuring. Hungry.

"This is… dangerous, Maddie with the purple hair. You make me feel like a reckless teenager. Or about a hundred years too old," he said grimly.

He took a harsh breath, jamming a hand through his hair. "Either way it's a bad thing."

Maddie started to answer, but her cell phone rang, her computer screen lit up, and a voice called from out in the hall.

And all the bad things happened at once.

Chapter Six

The phone in the room rang. Maddie's cell phone screeched. The doorbell rang in two harsh peals.

None of it was coincidence. How could it be, when her wrists were lighting up with long glowing strands of energy that twisted around her, warning of danger.

Gabriel's eyes narrowed. "I definitely want a piece of that technology," he muttered. "Whatever it is."

Not going to happen in this lifetime, Maddie thought. *And you've never even imagined technology like this.* "Whatever. I'll get the phone. You handle the door."

When she answered her cell, Izzy was on the other end, his voice cool and emotionless.

When he got distant like that, it meant things were really bad. "Get down here to the catering office. Bring your laptop. I have code for you to override. And keep Gabe with you. Move," he snapped.

Gabe was closing the door when Maddie broke off the call. He shoved on a high-tech earbud and scowled at her. The frown made him look dangerous.

And absolutely gorgeous.

Great. Another alpha male in her life.

But Gabe wasn't any of her business. *Get back to the spread sheets and computer code, Maddie girl. Sooner done the better. This is getting way too complicated. You're the one with nada social skills, remember?*

Gabe crossed to the couch and pulled on a tailored navy blazer that made him look like the CEO of a Fortune 500 company. *Talk about a chameleon*, Maddie thought.

"Who was at the door?"

"Room service. And an Elvis impersonator. Clearly someone wants to keep us distracted," he said curtly.

Maddie didn't even think about the food delivery. She grabbed her laptop, feeling the sense of warning grow. "That was Izzy on my cell. We need to get down to the catering department ASAP. There's a code to override."

"That's off a side corridor on the hotel mezzanine level." Gabe adjusted his small silver earbud and nodded. "But first you need to ditch the earring. Dangerous thing in a close quarters confrontation." He gently removed the earring and shook his head. "Teague should

142

have told you that."

"He did. I ignored him."

"Of course you did." Gabe sighed. "Now do something about those."

Maddie looked down.

Hell.

The lights were moving again, snaking over her shoulders in a restless dance. She turned away and took a deep breath, summoning up the balance that was still so new to her. She thought about Lyon and all he had taught her, using his patience and calm strength to soften the blow of hard discoveries.

She called up the memory of his face. His rugged body.

The lights stopped dancing and slowly faded.

Gabriel watched intently. "I'm going to get a piece of that technology. Count on it."

"It's a free country," Maddie muttered. "Now can we go?"

*

Half a dozen people were clustered outside the catering office. Gabriel strode right through the middle of the crowd, which quickly parted for him. Maddie saw Izzy at the end of the corridor and sprinted toward him.

A dog sat next to Izzy, motionless in front of the nearest locker. Maddie didn't know what kind of threat was indicated. Nuclear. Biohazard. Even something electromagnetic. It was a waste of her time to speculate, so she didn't bother.

"What do you need?"

"Scan that lock. It's digital. I keep picking up new number sequences, as if the code is being changed randomly."

Maddie pulled out her laptop and knelt in front of the locker. Dimly she sensed Gabriel move down behind her, his shoulder at her back. She was glad for the warmth and the unexpected sense of protection. Then she slid deep, focused on the task before her.

Numbers played through her head. Sequence possibilities.

But something made her feel cold. She looked up and her vision blurred.

A bright blue wave of color washed over the corridor at the edge of Maddie's vision. She shook her head, glancing back toward the catering office and the anxious crowd of workers. Nothing blue anywhere.

The image faded.

Maddie frowned and went back to work on the lock scan.

The job took her six minutes, and that was five minutes longer than she had ever taken before. She checked her code one more time. Her hands flexed. She hit the enter button.

A loud siren screeched inside the metal locker door.

"I did it right," Maddie called out angrily. She worked back through all the steps of her analysis. And then she hit enter again.

The siren stopped and the locker door slid open. Izzy nudged her aside, with the dog right beside him. "Get her back, Gabe," he ordered. "Get everyone back."

Maddie rubbed her neck and stepped to one side, feeling empty and drained now that her work was done. Izzy had warned her about the sense of letdown after a job, but it still caught her by surprise.

"I'm calling in backup. Gabe, give me a hand here, will you?"

Maddie felt a kick of emptiness when Gabe moved back to Izzy's big duffel back at the far corridor.

Blue.

When she looked down, something glowed along her hands and over her chest. Gabe was talking with Izzy, the dog still alert beside them. Maddie blinked, off balance, and a shape hurtled from the narrow cross corridor, hitting her hard and knocking her sideways.

Big, oily waves of blue surrounded her. She felt hard hands jerk her back into an open locker. She fought, shoving the Mace above her and spraying hard. Someone called her name while her neck burned.

And then she collapsed.

Chapter Seven

"Maddie, can you hear me?"

Her throat burned. She felt as if a truck was backing over her head.

"Open your eyes and talk to me, damn it."

Coughing, Maddie forced open her eyes. Gabe's face, very worried, loomed over her. "What?" she croaked.

He took a slow breath, and the heat of his body washed over her. His finger brushed her cheek. "How many fingers?"

She squinted up through the blurred lights. "Twenty-five."

"Funny, Einstein. Answer the question."

Maddie focused again. "Three. And a half."

"Excellent." He moved his hand, brushing a strand of purple hair from her face.

"What happened?"

"We got the roommate."

"Don't understand. What roommate?" Sound came back slowly. Maddie saw two police dogs and a man carried away under armed escort. "Who… was he?"

"Kade. He was dressed in a Blue Man costume, watching everything we did. He worked birthday parties and special events here in the hotel. The costume made a perfect disguise. How did you spot him?"

Maddie didn't have a clue. Mostly it had been instinct. And the lights, of course. "Not sure. Just luck."

"Close your eyes and rest. You've had a busy day. A medical team is headed up."

"Don't want to… rest. Want coffee. Breakfast too. Eggs. Biscuits and gravy. Chocolate cake."

Gabe muttered under his breath. "Forget the coffee."

"Kiss my—ashes," Maddie answered shakily.

"Anytime you want," Gabe said. "You name the place. I'll be there." His lips grazed her forehead. Maddie thought he said something else.

But she was shaking now. And she couldn't seem to focus. Her eyes closed. Dimly she felt Gabe's arm slide under her shoulders.

Breakfast would have to wait.

*

Gabe watched the team work over Maddie. "She's good, Teague. But she's way too young for this work."

"She's almost twenty. And she probably has more street sense than either of us," Izzy answered flatly. "Don't worry about Maddie Munro."

"Take care of her. I'll be keeping an eye on both of you." Gabe pulled on his pack and frowned. "What about those lights of hers? Is it new technology I should know about?"

Izzy's face was unreadable. "Don't know what you mean."

"Like hell you don't."

"Listen, Gabe, you know I can't discuss this. Let it go. Maddie is… different. She is as smart as they come, but her life has always been complicated. Better not get involved."

"But I am involved. And I'll be in touch."

Gabe watched a gurney roll down the hall and wondered at how small and fragile Maddie looked beneath the white sheet. The purple hair made her look young and hard at the same time.

It wasn't over, he thought.

Not even close.

Chapter Eight

Maddie listened to the whine of the airplane motors, feeling anxious the way she always did when she flew. The medicine she had been given at the hospital helped. So did her exhaustion after the briefing that afternoon.

But she couldn't relax. The report was done. Izzy was wrapping up the final details.

And she was here staring out the window. Thinking about Gabe.

He hadn't said goodbye. When she woke up, he was gone. No word, nothing. And that made her angry, as well as impossibly empty.

Let him go, Maddie girl. He's way beyond your league.

Izzy leaned over and set a brown paper bag on the armrest beside her. "Stop muttering under your breath. We aren't going to crash."

"Tell my stomach that."

"Focus on something else. Read a book on that new tablet I got you. Take up knitting."

"I'm considering it." Maddie wasn't joking. There were cool things that she wouldn't mind making.

"I'll believe that when I see it. Meanwhile, this is for you."

She frowned at the bag. "What is it?"

"Beats me. Open it and find out."

She pulled off the tape and unfolded the paper and immediately was hit with dark aromas. Light citrus mingled with clove and smoke. *Coffee.*

"Gabe left it for you. He was sorry he couldn't hang around."

Maddie swallowed, cradling the bag with fingers that trembled just a little. "He told you that?"

Izzy nodded. "He said not to take it out until you were in the air." Izzy rubbed his neck. "Gabe is important, Maddie. And the life he leads is complicated. Maybe I should say the lives he leads."

"I got that idea. But it's no business of mine." She didn't let go of the bag, with its rich, seductive smells. The cold feeling of emptiness began to lift and she could almost hear Gabe's laughter as he thought of her opening the gift. "None of my business at all."

"You sure about that?"

"I just told you, didn't I?"

Izzy watched her face. "You did a good job back in Vegas. We couldn't have wrapped this up so fast without you. The Senator sends his thanks."

"Hoorah." There was no warmth in her voice.

Izzy shook his head and turned away, typing the last of his report.

When Maddie looked down there were no lights on her arms. They were gone in the aftermath of the confrontation, maybe lost in her general exhaustion.

Fine. One less thing to worry about.

She watched clouds race past the small window and yawned, wondering where Gabriel was and what her next job would be. She wondered whether Lyon would be part of her work when she got back to England.

She blew out a breath. And then she saw the little brown envelope taped to the side of the bag.

"Why don't you read it?" Izzy murmured.

"Go away, Teague."

He laughed and went back to his typing and Maddie opened the card slowly, not sure what she expected to see or even what she wanted to see.

The letters were bold and black, racing across the plain brown paper.

Don't drink it all at once or you'll end up back in the hospital.

Maddie bit back a laugh.

He knew her too well already.

Stay safe, Maddie Munro.

I'll find you. One day when you least expect it, I'll be there. You can make us coffee and see what comes next.

Because whatever this is, it's not over.

Maddie really did laugh at that. The sudden sound of her own laughter made her feel giddy and complicated and unbelievably alive.

The lights swirled up then, wrapped along her wrists and over her arms. The colors and texture were different now, she realized. Darker. More complex.

A new tendril of patterned lines appeared, working its way amid the others, restless and complicated, twining with the old. Maddie gave up trying to control it and simply enjoyed the beautiful, swirling patterns.

Maybe that was part of life.

Or maybe it was growing up. Maddie didn't know where she was going, but she knew this thing.

Gabe would be back.

She would savor his coffee while she watched and waited.

And she was going to enjoy every moment of this crazy, unpredictable journey of discovery that lay before her.

13Thirty Books

Exciting Thrillers, Heart-Warming Romance,
Mind-Bending Horror, Sci-Fantasy
and
Educational Non-Fiction

The Third Hour

The Third Hour is an original spin on the religious-thriller genre, incorporating elements of science fiction along with the religious angle. Its strength lies in this originality, combined with an interesting take on real historical figures, who are made a part of the experiment at the heart of the novel, and the fast pace that builds.

Ripper – A Love Story

"Queen Victoria would not be amused--but you will be by this beguiling combination of romance and murder. Is the Crown Prince of England really Jack the Ripper? His wife would certainly like to know… and so will you."
Diana Gabaldon, New York Times Best Selling Author

Heather Graham's Haunted Treasures

Presented together for the first time, New York Times Bestselling Author, Heather Graham brings back three tales of paranormal love and adventure.

Heather Graham's Christmas Treasures

New York Times Bestselling Author, Heather Graham brings back three out-of-print Christmas classics that are sure to inspire, amaze, and warm your heart.

Zodiac Lovers Series

Zodiac Lovers is a series of romantic, gay, paranormal novelettes. In each story, one of the lovers has all the traits of his respective zodiacal sign.

Never Fear

Shh... Something's Coming

Never Fear – Phobias

Everyone Fears Something

Never Fear – Christmas Terrors

He sees you when you're sleeping ...

More Than Magick

Why me? Recent college grad Scott Madison, has been recruited (for reasons that he will eventually understand) by the wizard Arion and secretly groomed by his ostensible friend and mentor, Jake Kesten. But his training hasn't readied him to face Vraasz, a being who has become powerful enough to destroy the universe and whose first objective is the obliteration of Arion's home world. Scott doesn't understand why he was the chosen one or why he is traveling the universe with a ragtag group of individuals also chosen by Arion. With time running out, Scott discovers that he has a power that can defeat Vraasz. If only he can figure out how to use it.

Stop Saying Yes – Negotiate!

Stop Saying Yes - Negotiate! is the perfect "on the go" guide for all negotiations. This easy-to-read, practical guide will enable you to quickly identify the other side's tactics and strategies allowing you to defend yourself ensuring a better negotiation for your side and theirs.

13Thirtybooks.com
facebook.com/13thirty